PRAI[SE FOR]
A HOUS[E AT THE]
BOTTOM OF A LAKE

"Malerman tests the waters of love and magic, and what it means
to face both as a teenager, in this beautifully crafted horror story."
LIVIUS NEDIN, BOOKED. PODCAST

"In *A House at the Bottom of a Lake*, Josh Malerman gives us exactly
that. And it is as weird and as deeply disturbing as you might
expect. From the teenage characters' awkwardness, so expertly
rendered, to their pushing farther and farther into the submerged
house, the story unfolds on a level that is achingly deep yet instantly
accessible. Malerman is a helluva writer and as cool as a cucumber
throughout, and the story is unsettlingly beautiful."
JOHN F.D. TAFF, author of *The End in All Beginnings*

"An intimate dive into eerie, ethereal
—and elegantly human—waters."
DREAD CENTRAL

"Never has something so scary been so much fun. If you don't
fall in love with the two kids in *A House at the Bottom of a Lake*,
you don't have a heart. Malerman has given us a new reason to
be afraid of water—and a new reason to explore it."
DARK MOON DIGEST

"Josh Malerman lures you into his nightmare like a predator.
A House at the Bottom of a Lake is raising the bar for several classic
horror tropes. Malerman is a daring and crafty storyteller."
DEAD END FOLLIES

"Josh Malerman expertly conjures a fairy tale nostalgia of first love,
and we follow along, all too willingly, ignoring the warning signs
even as the fear takes hold."
JOSHUA CHAPLINSKY, LITREACTOR.COM

A This Is Horror Publication
www.ThisIsHorror.co.uk

ISBN: 978-1-910471-01-2

The right of Josh Malerman to be identified as the author of
this work has been asserted by him in accordance with the
Copyright, Designs and Patents Act 1988.

First published in 2016 by This Is Horror

Editor-in-Chief: Michael David Wilson
Cover art and design: Pye Parr

A HOUSE AT THE BOTTOM OF A LAKE

JOSH MALERMAN

ABOUT THE AUTHOR

Josh Malerman is the author of the award-winning novel *Bird Box* and the lead singer for the rock band The High Strung. Malerman currently lives in Ferndale, Michigan.

Photograph by Allison Laakko.

For the craziness of courtship.
For the heart of a house of horrors aflame.
For Allison.

1

It's the best first date I've ever heard of.

Amelia smiled big and nodded.

"Yes?" James said, not sure he'd read her right.

How can I say no?

"How can I say no? Canoeing with a stranger? Yes. I'd love to."

Both seventeen. Both afraid. But both saying yes.

James ran sweaty hands through his brown hair then wiped them again on his apron. This wasn't the first time he'd seen her in his father's store. It was the fourth.

"My name is Amelia," she said, wondering if he already knew that, if he'd found her online.

"James," he said and smiled, too. "And wow was I nervous to ask you out."

"Really?" She asked it earnestly, but knew he was. The fidgeting revealed that. She was anxious, too. "Why?"

James snorted a single awkward chuckle.

"You know ... boy girl ... people meet... I don't know! It's scary!"

Amelia laughed. It felt good to have a boy ask her out. God, it felt *great*. How long had it been since she'd gone on a date? And here, at the very onset of summer, it felt ... natural.

A new day.

A new season.

And a yes to a stranger who'd asked her to go canoeing for a first date.

"So here's the idea," James said, checking over his shoulder for his Dad. "My uncle has a place on a lake—"

"You said so, yep."

"Yeah, but there's a *second* lake, off the first one, that *nobody* uses. I mean ... some people do, but there won't be, like, a ton of speedboats. We can actually paddle right up to the shoreline, to the base of the mountains. And we'll pretty much have them all to ourselves. The mountains."

"Sounds great," Amelia said, hooking her thumbs into the belt loops of her jean shorts. She arched her back beneath her yellow tank top. She worried she was augmenting her breasts too much. So she slumped. Then she worried that she was slumping.

James was even more self-conscious than she was. This being his father's hardware store, he was sure Amelia would have second thoughts if she hung around too long. *Is this his future?* She might think. A girl said that to him once. Asked if this was his future. James didn't want Amelia asking that. Didn't want her walking away. If she was thinking anything like he was, she was already seeing a future together, a life rolling out rug-like from their first date. He saw them laughing on the first lake, kissing on the second, getting married in a canoe, Amelia giving birth in a canoe ...

"Saturday then," she said and for a crazy second he thought she was saying they should get married on Saturday. His cheeks flushed. He became very aware of that. His cheeks. Then his whole body. He worried suddenly that he didn't workout enough. Worried that she was going to leave here thinking about the paunch beneath his apron and not the mountains he'd tried to distract her with.

And yet, he managed a smile. Even found some confidence in his voice.

"Yes, Saturday. Nine a.m. Wanna meet here?"

"Here?" She looked up and down the aisle of rubber hoses, hose clamps, and bolts. Maybe this was the moment then, when she realized the scope of the situation, the job he had, his future.

"Unless you wanna meet somewhere else? I don't care."

"No no," Amelia said, attempting to appear casual while worrying that she was being suddenly indecisive in front of him. "Here is fine. Here is great. Saturday. Nine."

James stuck his hand out for her to shake, then realized how awkward that was.

Here is great.

He brought his hand back just as she reached hers out to shake it. Then she lowered hers, too.

"Great."

"Great."

They stared at one another, neither certain how to end their first conversation. A muzak version of a love song from the 1980s played through the hardware store's equally archaic speakers. Both felt the cheese.

"Bye," James said, then scurried back down the aisle.

He nearly knocked a box of garden floodlights from the shelf. He didn't look back at Amelia as he fixed it. Instead, he set out to find a customer, anybody who looked like they might need help. But when he was far enough away from her, he wished he *had* looked back.

He just wanted to see her face once more.

Saturday, he thought. *You'll see her again.*

Outside, walking quick to her car, Amelia replayed James's offer. She loved it.

It's the best first date I've ever heard of.

And it didn't hurt that James had kind eyes. A kind face and kind voice, too.

It wasn't until she got behind the wheel of her used yellow Omni did she realize she hadn't bought what she'd gone in to the store to buy. A new hose.

She thought of going back in.

No. She decided. *Maybe a date was what you came here for.*

She started the car.

2

"Cool," Amelia said. "It's green."

It *was* cool. A green canoe with brown trim. It looked like the kind of canoe you'd find in a history book, two Native Americans seated inside.

"It's sturdy, too," James's Uncle Bob said. His jean shorts and open flannel were straight out of 1995. "But that doesn't mean it won't tip."

Amelia and James exchanged glances. They were already ankle deep in the cold water. They hardly knew one another at all.

"We won't stand up in her," James said. "I know better."

"I do, too." Amelia said.

"You've canoed before?" Uncle Bob asked her.

Amelia blushed.

"I wouldn't say I've *canoed*, you know, but I've been in one. Yeah. Is that canoeing?"

Uncle Bob laughed and lifted the paddles from inside the boat.

"These are solid cherry wood. Don't ask why. Trish wanted them that way. I don't think she's used them since we got them. But, heck, you two get to use some pretty fancy paddles."

Bob eyed the cooler James had already placed in the canoe.

"I don't mind if you two have some beers out there, but be careful, all right?" He turned to Amelia. "How old are you?"

"Seventeen."

Bob considered this. But not for very long.

"A couple of seventeen-year-olds," he said. His eyes got glassy. Like he was remembering seventeen. "Awesome."

When James got to the front of the canoe he was shin deep. He stepped over the edge and sat down on the front bench. Amelia got into the back behind him.

"Thank you for this, Bob," Amelia said.

"Absolutely." He placed a sandaled foot on the back end of the canoe. "Now go be seventeen."

He pushed them out into the water.

3

"This is the lake," James said. Then he snapped his fingers, like trying to catch the words as they left him. *Of course* it was the lake.

"It's gorgeous," Amelia said.

James was paddling on the right side of the canoe. Amelia paddled on the left and steered.

Her eyes traveled to the rippling surface of the water.

It was a great blue, the kind of blue you painted.

Amelia felt like she *was* painting; the oar as her brush. As though all this beauty fanned out from the simple motions she and James made.

"What do you think is down there?' she asked. Then wished she hadn't. The question made it sound like she was scared. *What's in there?* "I mean ... what kind of fish?"

She didn't have the heart to tell James that his shorts were hanging a little low and she could see the very top of his plumber's crack.

Plumber's crack. Hardware store. This made her smile.

"All kinds," James said, not sure of the answer. "Bass ... I think."

He wanted to tell her there was something magical in this lake. A buried treasure. A mysterious shipwreck. A monster.

He also regretted sitting up-front. He couldn't see her from here.

He turned around to face her.

His eyes were hidden behind his sunglasses, his fair brown hair wet with sweat from the paddling. And beyond him was the endless blue. But no ... *not* endless. The lake was bordered neatly by the shoreline, the toes of the feet of mountains. And the mountains were covered with trees.

There were many homes at the base of the mountains. A-frames and ranches. Decks where the families no doubt sat outside, drank coffee, watched the sun rise and set on the lake. Amelia wondered what kind of animals lived between the trees. Between the houses.

A boat's engine revved, and James looked ahead again. Amelia saw a speedboat far to the right, cresting the shoreline as if creating it. Watching the four people in bikinis and briefs on board, she was surprised to find she liked the idea of the canoe better. The green canoe with the brown trim. Old school. She looked to the cooler between them, knew that James had brought some beers. Some sandwiches. It felt so much … classier. Paddling instead of revving. Talking instead of howling. Seeing instead of racing by.

A sudden shrill scream and both James and Amelia saw one of the girls in the speedboat laughing, leaning over the back edge, too close to the motor, flailing her arms toward the wake.

She was drunk. Carefree. Having a blast.

James worried that Amelia might think the speedboat looked like more fun. It *did* look fun. And here he was sweating in his Uncle's canoe while some other guys with a real boat were making girls scream all over the lake.

He looked over his shoulder, trying to gauge her enthusiasm.

She was beautiful. Just gorgeous. Truly. Her auburn hair looked especially vivid against the backdrop of blue lake behind her. He wasn't sure exactly where he'd found the nerve to ask her out. He just did it. The canoe, the lake, all of this just came pouring out of him because it was the first fun thing he thought of. And now, he needed more nerve. More confidence. Where did it go?

Was she having fun?

James turned away from her, looked ahead again.

Something jumped in the water. James pointed.

"Did you see that?" he called over his shoulder.

"No, but I heard it."

"That was *big.*"

"How big?"

The ripples left behind spread wide.

"I don't know. Like the size of a loaf of bread?"

Amelia snorted a stifled laugh. Then she snickered. Then she laughed outright.

"The size of a loaf of bread? What the hell does that mean?"

She laughed harder.

James laughed, too.

"I swear. It was like a loaf of rye bread just leapt right out of the water."

Amelia almost told him that made her hungry. But really it didn't. It made her think of soggy bread.

Jesus, she thought. *You're just thinking of things to say. And guys notice that! Guys notice when girls are just trying to think of something to say.*

James thought, *Shit. Those guys in that boat are thrilling the bikinis off those girls and I'm bringing up rye bread. Come on!*

Then James ducked to pick something up at his feet and Amelia saw the horizon split by his hunched form. The mountains fanned out on either side of the canoe's tip. It was incredible.

James popped back up, and between his forefinger and thumb he held a spider.

"A spider!" he said, and Amelia could see it was a big one. Big enough.

She searched the floor near her shoes. Searched the towel she sat on.

"Shit," she said.

"You don't like him?"

"No ... I mean ... it's not that I don't *like* him ..."

"Scared of spiders? A little? I'll get rid of him."

"No! Where would you put him?"

James looked to either side of the canoe.

"The water?"

"No, no. That's terrible. I can't live knowing that he was sent out to sea because of me."

Can't live? Out to sea? Amelia felt like everything she said was wrong. Didn't define her. Didn't explain her to James.

"Well, shoot. Looks like he stays, then."

But he wanted to help her. Didn't want her to be scared. The guys in the speedboat probably killed spiders all day.

"Okay," Amelia said. "But maybe keep an eye on him for me?"

James set the spider down on the tip of the canoe. He pointed ahead.

"Look there," he said. "That's the entrance to the second lake. No homes at all on that one."

Amelia glanced to a roof jutting from the trees at the base of the mountains. As if it were sinking. Or hiding.

"Sounds cool," she said.

They paddled toward the second lake.

4

Amelia didn't think it was possible, it was, after all, *very* unlikely, but the second lake *was* more beautiful than the first.

And more remote.

It was smaller by a third of the size, she guessed, and the shores were so crowded with trees that it appeared there was no land there at all.

Like the water is supported by trees, a lake on stilts.

And the water!

Gorgeous. Not like the tropical beaches she'd seen in pictures, even better than that. The clearest she'd ever seen.

"This is …" she started to say but stopped. She stopped paddling, too. Laid the oar across her legs, rolled up her sleeves, and just *saw*.

James continued to paddle, but slow, taking it in, too.

Amelia listened to the canoe cut the cool surface, the only sound out here, as if all the fish were sleeping. She caught a reflection in the water, *her* reflection, her face a rippling disc amongst auburn straw.

The green body of the canoe looked like it belonged here, like it was a part of the second lake. Like it was made for it.

She looked ahead, silently thanking James, and saw he had his oar across his legs, too. He was looking to the right, she could see his profile clearly, and she was very glad she'd said yes to his offer.

"You hungry?" James asked, still looking to the right, to the shoreline of heavy trees.

He was hungry. Had been since before they set off. Wanted to show her the lakes first, wanted to wait until they were out here in the middle of the second one. If it turned out they had nothing to talk about? Well, fine. He had food. And if they did have something to talk about, they could talk over lunch.

"Yes," Amelia said.

James carefully swung his feet over the bench and Amelia recalled Uncle Bob warning them about tipping. She saw it then, the two of them sprawling into the water, arms out, the canoe sinking, no boats out here to help them. They'd have to swim to shore. They'd lose the cooler, their things.

Facing her now on the bench, James went to his knees and the canoe actually did rock. Amelia gripped the sides. James paused, while mid-reach for the cooler.

The canoe stabilized.

They looked at each other. They laughed.

"Sorry," James said. "That wasn't very smart."

"That was close."

But was it? It was certainly enough to scare her.

"Sorry," he said again.

"No. Don't worry. I just imagined us drowning is all."

Was that a dumb joke?

James felt dumb, too.

"Turkey sandwich?" he asked. "Chips? Water?"

"Sounds good. Sounds like a meal deal."

Another dumb joke. Who would bring up a meal deal while surrounded by everything that was so much the opposite of a meal deal?

But James smiled. Then he pulled out two sandwiches wrapped in foil, two bottles of water, and two bags of plain chips. He handed Amelia hers. Then he rose, carefully, and got back on the bench.

"You got a problem with your hose?" James asked her.

Amelia laughed with her mouth full and coughed from it.

"You okay?"

"Yes," she said, then swallowed. "And yes, I do have a problem with my hose. I totally forgot to buy a new one when I was in your store."

"It's not my store."

James wished he hadn't said it that way. He hadn't decided yet if he wanted to tell Amelia that his dad owned the place. Did she already know?

"What's wrong with the hose?" he asked her.

"It's got holes in it."

"Are you sure it isn't the clamp?"

"What's a clamp?"

A bird flew low to the water, many feet away. James looked at Amelia's legs.

"The clamp that holds two hoses together. Is it two hoses?"

"It is, yeah."

"Probably the clamp, then." He took a bite of his sandwich. The bird rose high up again. Amelia's skin looked so clean to him, so soft. "Did you see an actual hole in one of the hoses?"

"I think so."

"Then it might not be the clamp. I can fix it either way."

"You can?"

"Sure. Or I'll show you how and you can do it. It's simple, if you think about it. Fixing stuff. There are only so many parts to a thing, you know? So you just start figuring out which part is the broken part."

"Okay."

An eagle flew above them. Flew to the shoreline. Settled at the top of a tree.

"Oh man," James said, setting his lunch on top of the cooler. "I bet we can see it up close."

Even from as far as they were, Amelia thought she could make out a nest in the treetop. A big wicker basket harboring the bird.

"Let's do it."

James was already turning around.

"You ready?" he called to her.

"Ready."

They paddled toward the trees, quickly. The eagle remained in the nest. It seemed to be watching them approach. When they were close enough, James pushed his oar against the water and the canoe turned slightly, gliding to a partial stop near the shoreline.

James turned to Amelia and placed a finger over his lips.

But Amelia had to say something.

"Holy *shit*," she whispered. "I've never seen one ... *so close!*"

This was good, James thought. An eagle could be as exciting as a speedboat.

"It's incredible," he said.

Amelia wished she had brought a camera. Then she decided it was okay that she didn't have one. She could bring one next time. Then she realized she was already thinking of next time.

They studied the bird for a long time. Eventually it flew away, hunting, and Amelia followed its path, its trajectory, until something far beneath it caught her eye.

"What's that?" she asked.

James looked, expecting to see another bird.

"What's what?"

"That," Amelia pointed it out with an oar.

"I don't see anything."

"It's ... a little bridge, maybe?"

James held a hand over his eyes and squinted where she was pointing.

"I don't remember any bridge out here. And I still don't see what you mean."

"You see that dark evergreen there?"

"Which one?"

"It's tall. Taller than the—"

"Yeah, I see it."

"Okay, now go down to its base and to the left like … one … two … three trees."

James did. He saw it.

"Oh wow. I have no idea. Oh wait. I do know what that is."

"What?"

"It's like a tiny stretch of road. Concrete. I think it's for whoever maintains the lakes. Like a service drive."

"Ah."

James smiled.

"You wanna check it out, don't you?"

Amelia shrugged. She didn't want to say no to anything. Not today.

"Yeah, I mean. Why not?"

"Yeah," James said. "Okay. So do I."

They paddled toward the concrete patch of road almost buried in the trees at the shoreline.

5

"What did you do on some of your other first dates?" James called over his shoulder.

"What?"

"What were some of your other first dates like?"

"Nothing like this," she called. "Movies. Dinner."

Good, James thought.

"The movies is a bad first date," he said.

"Yeah."

"Even if the movie is good."

"Yeah."

Amelia considered saying something clever like, *you can learn a lot about somebody by sitting in the dark with them for two hours.* But she didn't say it because she didn't really believe it.

"I had one date," she said, paddling, steering, "where this guy took me to his parents' ranch in Obega."

"That sounds all right."

"His parents were there."

"Wow. You met his parents on the first date?"

"Yep. I did."

James laughed. Amelia laughed. They were free about their laughter but there was something anxious about it, too.

"You see that tangle of brush just below the concrete?" she asked.

"I do, yeah."

"What is it hiding?"

They were close enough now to see there was a tunnel under the concrete. The colors red and neon green, black and orange popped out at them.

Graffiti. A lot of it. Strange phrases that read like nonsense to them but must have meant something to someone else.

"Punks," Amelia said and then wished she hadn't. That was something her mom would've said. Why did it sound funny before it came out? Didn't she know what funny was?

"What?"

She wasn't going to repeat it.

"Closer," she said instead. "Let's get closer."

"Yep."

The water was darker along the shoreline, shadowed by the trees. Amelia wondered if it was deeper here, if the water that ran through the tunnel went really deep.

"I had the worst first date ever," James said, still paddling.

"Oh yeah?"

"Yeah. I asked a girl to go bowling and she said yes and my plan was to invite some friends, make a night of it. But nobody could go, nobody said yes, and so I ended up going bowling with a girl I really didn't know at all."

"You're pretty good at that."

James looked over his shoulder. Amelia smiled.

"Well, I don't ask a lot of girls out, if that's what you mean."

"I just meant that you're pretty good at hanging out with somebody you don't know."

"Am I?"

"Yeah."

Amelia smiled. James wanted to kiss her.

"Thanks," he said. And he meant it. "So we went bowling and the girl was nice but also really shy and so I had a hard time talking to her. I asked her about things, but it wasn't easy. Then it was her turn to bowl and she was walking up the lane and she slipped and fell and broke her arm."

"Whoa!"

"At the elbow."

"Oh man."

"Yeah. It was terrible."

They were close enough to the tunnel to see someone had painted a bloated, veined penis with googly eyes.

"Punks," James said, and Amelia wished she had repeated it.

They were as close as they could go without entering the tunnel. So they stopped rowing. They drifted. They stared into the tunnel.

"Hey," James said. "That might be another lake on the other side there."

Amelia saw what he meant.

"And you've never been over there?"

"No. I don't think the canoe would even fit through there."

Amelia had a vision of the two of them stuck inside the tunnel. A bloated, veiny penis with googly eyes rising from the water.

"I bet we'll fit," she said.

"Yeah?"

"Yeah."

"All right," James said. "Let's try it."

6

Straight away the canoe scraped against the concrete walls of the tunnel and James thought about his Uncle Bob.

Shit. The paint.

The green paint. Chipping.

The canoe fit. But just.

It was so tight they couldn't use their paddles. Couldn't even lay the paddles across their knees. James laid his on the floor instead. Amelia did the same. They pushed their way through the tunnel with their fingers and palms.

They didn't speak of not doing it. They didn't speak of backing out.

Amelia was surprised when James pulled a flashlight from his backpack. It underscored how dark it was in here.

It felt like they were going to get stuck, over and over, too tight, the tunnel narrowing. But the tunnel *didn't* narrow, and they didn't get stuck. Just more of the scraping and chipping.

Halfway through they had to duck and two-thirds of the way they had to *really* duck, until their shoulders were between their knees.

"Like a coffin," Amelia said. It sounded funnier in her head.

James was breathing hard. It wasn't easy work.

"Look at this one," he said, bent completely at the waist, shining the light on the wall, an inch from the side of the canoe.

It was a stick figure woman with enormous tits. Something like milk was squirting out of them. A second stick figure woman was on her knees, tongue out, to accept it.

"Wow," Amelia said. "An artist tunnel. Horny vandals."

James liked hearing her say that word.

Horny.

A foot from the drawing was the word 'PRICKS' in pink.

They laughed. And their laughter echoed in the tunnel.

"Can we stop for a second?" James asked.

"Here?"

"Yeah. It's killing me."

"Yeah."

James turned off the light. They both breathed hard. Amelia had a vision of him turning the light on again, under his face, monster lighting, revealing grotesque graffitied lips and eyebrows.

"I had another weird first date," James said in the dark.

"Weirder than this?"

"There used to be a coffee shop in town called Rita's. Remember Rita's?"

"Yeah."

"Yeah. I used to read books there all the time. I really got into Agatha Christie and—"

"Wait. Wait. Agatha Christie?"

"Yeah."

"My grandmother reads Agatha Christie."

"She's great."

"Really?"

"Yeah."

"Okay."

"I mean it."

"I believe you. So what happened?"

"Well, this *girl* was reading Agatha Christie too and she'd come talk to me about it. Which book was my favorite. That kind of thing."

"Sounds like a good start."

"I guess. And then she asked me out."

"Where?"

The echoes of their voices were sharp, high-pitched. Their breathing sounded like the breathing of four people, not two.

"She asked me if I wanted to hang out that night, after the coffee shop closed. That's all she said. And I said okay. But then she walked back to her table and it all felt really weird, you know? Because she was reading at her table and I was reading at mine and here we were, supposed to go on this date I guess, but we weren't talking to each other at all. You know? I wanted to leave the coffee shop but I felt bad about it, like I'd be standing her up or something. So I read eighty more pages of the book than I had planned. And the whole time she's reading hers across the coffee shop. And the second they closed she walked right up to me and said, 'Ready?' And I said yeah. She said we should go to her place and watch a movie."

"Wow," Amelia said. "Was she wearing a hospital bracelet?"

"What?"

"What happened next?"

"We went to her house. We went into the basement. We sat on opposite ends of the couch."

"She had a sitting close to you problem?"

James laughed.

"Yes she did! And she says, 'Have you ever seen *The Woodsman?*' And let me ask you, Amelia, have *you* ever seen *The Woodsman?*"

"Oh boy. You did *not* watch that movie on a first date."

"We did," James said. "We did."

Amelia laughed. Then she laughed again.

"Ready?" James asked. "I think I'm rested."

"Yep."

They planted their palms against the slick walls and pushed forward again. The scraping and chipping returned immediately.

Ahead, sunlight. But no view. Not yet.

They pushed. Amelia felt sweat dripping down the sides of her breasts, the sides of her belly.

They were able to sit up a little more again. Halfway.

"Almost there," James called.

The canoe got stuck.

Felt like it wasn't going to move.

"Shit," James said.

"Shit."

"Let's just do it. Let's give it a really hard push."

"Are you worried about scratching the canoe? Are you worried about the paint?"

"Yes."

"What are we gonna do about it?"

"I'll get some paint from my dad's store."

"Your dad's store?"

"Shit."

"What?"

"I just didn't want to tell you that my Dad owns the hardware store I work at."

"Why didn't you want to tell me that?"

"You didn't know?"

"No. But that's great."

"I was worried you'd think that was my future."

"Really?"

Of course, that meant he was thinking about a future with her. She didn't know how that made her feel.

"Are you ready?" James asked.

Amelia was glad for the subject change. They both were.

"Ready."

They flattened their hands against the walls. A new sound announced itself; bent metal. The phrase sounded like a band to Amelia.

Bent Metal.

James grunted and shoved as hard as he could.

Water sloshed against the tip of the canoe. It sounded fresh, cold, new.

They gave it one more hard push and, with a deafening squawk, the canoe broke free.

Cool air washed over them and they fell back onto their benches, leaning back, as the canoe slid out of the tunnel on its own, propelled by their final thrust.

Neither went for their paddles as the canoe slowly drifted out onto the surface of a third lake.

"Holy shit," Amelia said.

"Yeah," James said. "Holy shit."

7

The third lake felt inhabited. Or like it once was. Or maybe it was just that whoever used the service drive came here often enough to leave some energy behind.

"Deliverance," Amelia said. But that was silly. They weren't in the backwoods of Tennessee. And besides, that's what everybody said when they were in a canoe and felt a little weird about their surroundings.

There shoreline was crowded with tall pines that rose from dark green shrubs.

The water was murky, as if the mud from the lake floor had come up to see who had cleared the tunnel.

"I can't believe my uncle never told me about this," James said.

But Amelia thought she understood. Given the grandeur and beauty of the first two lakes, there was no reason to ever visit this third one. It was an afterthought. The clogged gutter of an otherwise beautiful home.

And there was a smell to it, too. Not quite garbage, but like personal belongings no longer needed. Amelia had smelled something like it at estate sales with her mom and dad.

"That's it," Amelia said.

"What's it?" They were paddling again, going farther from the tunnel, getting closer to the middle of the new lake.

"It feels like we're seeing something we shouldn't be seeing. Something private."

James cocked his head to the sky.

"Do you smell that?" he asked.

"I think so," she said. But she wondered what he thought it was. "What do you smell?"

"*Old age!*" He turned around and smiled at her.

Amelia smiled, too. She thought of the first lake. Should they go back to it?

"It's not so bad," she said, wanting to remain positive. "If this was the first lake we saw today, I don't think it'd look so dismal."

"Really?"

"Yes. It's all about comparisons."

"I think I'd've felt the same."

"Even if we hadn't seen the other two?"

"But we did see the other two."

"We did."

It wasn't small, but it wasn't huge either; about half the size of the first lake and two-thirds that of the second. There were less trees at the shoreline and they could see where the mountains slipped coldly into the water. They were paddling toward them.

Unvisited.

The word seemed to float up and out of the water, slip wet into Amelia's mind.

"Are you hungry still?" James asked. "We didn't really finish our lunch."

The question was jarring, Amelia thought. Out of place. But why?

Because you guys were eating lunch on the second lake. This is the third lake now. Things are different here.

She looked over the edge of the canoe. A fish floated on its side, a foot below the surface.

Dead, Amelia thought.

But it was more like the fish was looking up, looking at her.

"I'm okay," she said, but the fish unnerved her. Was something wrong with the water? Dead fish in a lake was, of course, natural. But it was more about the look in the fish's eye, like they'd made actual eye contact, fish and girl.

"I'm always hungry," James said. "As a kid I used to eat two … *holy shit!*"

Amelia looked quick to James. She'd been thinking of the fish when he yelled. Was he yelling about the fish?

"What?" Amelia asked. Scared. "What?"

He lifted his paddle out of the water and Amelia did the same.

James was staring at the lake's surface, wide-eyed, too wide-eyed.

Amelia looked.

She saw it, too.

A roof.

"Oh God," she said. "Oh my *God*."

They drifted past it, over it, a small bird in its sky, a tiny airplane for two.

"Was that a …" James started but couldn't finish.

"Yes," Amelia said. "That was a *house*."

It was true then; they'd both seen it. A house. Submerged. A rooftop beneath the surface. And yet, it was so dark down there . . .

James snapped back first, jammed his paddle into the water, and started paddling in the opposite direction, driving the canoe in reverse. Amelia did the same.

Then they drifted.

Over the house again.

The house.

Underwater.

Without speaking, they gripped the edge of the canoe at the same time, their fingertips touching the chipped paint. Sunlight tap-danced across the surface, a glittering curtain, a welcoming, a reveal.

But not much of one.

"Oh my God," Amelia said again.

It's all she could think to say.

"It's huge," James said.

If the shingled roof was any indication, it was a big house.

Beneath them.

Underwater.

They looked at one another at the same time and it was stated silently that they were going to check it out. They were going to go into the water. No self-respecting seventeen-year-olds on a first date could paddle away from *this*.

But first, for a minute or two, for now ... they just stared.

8

"We've got a ladder," James said, shaking it loose from the lifejackets and towels on the floor of the canoe.

"So we can get back in," Amelia said. This was not a question. This was her accepting the turn the afternoon had taken.

The roof rippled with waves unseen, undulations beneath the surface.

Amelia started laughing. What else was there to do? Unless the roof was floating, there had to be a house beneath it. James joined her in laughing.

What else was there to do?

"It's a fucking *house!*" she said. Then she squealed because she was on a first date and they'd discovered something crazy enough to call magic.

James draped the ladder over the canoe's edge. When the rungs clacked against the chipped paint he felt a twinge of guilt. Uncle Bob. Did Uncle Bob know about this roof?

Still smiling, feeling the charge of discovery, Amelia looked across the lake to the entrance of the tunnel. A half-hole from here. Cartoonish, too. Like someone had painted it on a dip in the mountains.

It's not a real entrance, she thought. *It's a solid wall.* Then she shook the silly thought aside but couldn't shake a truer one.

The tunnel makes for a slow getaway.

She looked back to the submerged roof. James was shaking his head slowly side-to-side. He looked at her and they laughed again, lightly, in the way something uncanny can make someone laugh. Not funny. Impossible.

"All right" James said, gripping the rope ladder. "Who's going first?"

The individual rung looked like kindling in his hands. Amelia had a vision of the ladder erupting into flames. No easy way back into the canoe then, either.

But what unnecessary dark thoughts to have.

"I'll do it," she said. No wet blanket today.

James looked surprised.

"Really? Shouldn't I?"

"Why?"

"I don't know. Fine. You go first."

"No. You go first."

"No, no. Really."

"I think I need a minute to get used to the idea," she said. She was excited, but she was scared. There was more than just a 'tip of the iceberg' quality to the roof. Who knew the size and scope beneath it? "But we definitely *both* have to do it."

"I'm so glad you're saying that," James said. "We could just as easily paddle away and pretend this never happened, too."

"Could we?"

"Well, I ..."

No, he thought, looking into her bright eyes. Just then she looked very dry to him.

James scanned the shoreline. There was no sign of life. No angry old man to holler at them. No resident in sight to tell his Uncle Bob what he and the girl had been up to. It felt to James like they were in the center of a silent room. A room of their own.

He checked the surface of the water. He was looking for snapping turtles. Snakes. The bubbles of something breathing below.

What a terrible turn the date would take if James were to dive in and get bit by a moccasin. But the longer he stared at the surface the more the rippling roof looked like a painting. Oils. Like diving into *that,* into its false reality, would prove to be much worse than anything a snake could deliver.

"Amelia," he said, and he discovered he liked saying her name. *Amelia.* She was looking back at him, waiting for him to say whatever he was going to say. Her body looked smooth, pure, against the red of her bathing suit. He suddenly felt like he hadn't been looking at her enough. Her body. The curves, the slopes, the skin. "How do you think it got down there?"

"God's dollhouse."

"What?"

"I don't know."

"Did you just make that up?"

"Yeah."

"Sounded like a movie title."

"Haha. Thank you."

"I think it was built down there."

"Probably not."

"Had to be."

"I don't think so. I think it broke the ice."

"Ice?"

"Yeah. Someone tried to move it across the lake."

"Wow. That's interesting. But these lakes never ice over."

"Well, see. Someone should've told them that."

James smiled.

The canoe had shifted its position and the submerged rooftop was nearer the back now. On his knees, James used his paddle to bring them back to where they were. Amelia thought again of Uncle Bob's warning about tipping.

"Are you scared?" She asked.

"Um ..."

"Be honest."

"I'm always honest."

"Are you?"

"I mean ... yeah."

"Are you scared?"

She was smiling. The arched eyebrows-smile friends give each other before they enter the house of horrors at the county fair or press play on a particularly frightening movie.

Ready or not ... here we go.

"Yeah, sure. But not enough not to do it."

"Okay. Same here."

And what was there to be afraid of? In fact, after having spoken it, Amelia felt almost no fear at all. It was a submerged house, for crying out loud. It was *cool* was what it was.

And yet, looking at it, the house, the shingles seemed to move uniformly, as if it wasn't the surface of the water that created the illusion but something *beneath* the roof, rolling along its distance. Fish, perhaps. Or mice. As the roof sloped, its edges vanished into the murky shadows. Not only was Amelia unsure how large the house was, she wasn't even sure how big the *roof* was. Those same shadows continued, merged with the darkness that was the rest of the lake. She looked up, out, across the lake, and realized how big this third lake actually was. When you imagined yourself slipping into the water, imagined your tiny body engulfed by it, the lake looked a lot bigger.

"Is there anything in there that can bite us?"

"In the house?"

"No. The water."

"I really don't know. That's a bad answer, I know. If either of us should know, it's me. But ... I don't."

"It's okay. There's probably not. It's just a lake. It's not the ocean."

"Right."

"Okay."

"Okay. Here we go then."

He rose, suddenly, and Amelia's heart thudded bunny-like in her chest.

Here we go then.

"It'll be amazing," she said, trying to send some confidence his way.

James smiled at her. He was standing up. Balancing. When he removed his shirt, Amelia noticed how soft his chest looked. His white arms shined against the dark blue backdrop of the lake.

Then he dove in.

Amelia gripped the sides of the rocking canoe and looked over the edge.

As he sunk, the ripples created a blurry wall of white foam and bubbles. For a three-count Amelia couldn't see him.

It swallowed him, she thought.

James popped back up, his hair plastered wet to his head.

"Wow," he said, teeth chattering, treading. "It's really fucking cold."

Amelia didn't want to tell him how small he looked, treading the surface with the huge roof looming beneath him. She didn't want to tell him that he'd added scale to the sight.

"How long can you hold your breath?" she asked.

"I don't know. How long can someone hold their breath?"

"A minute or two I think."

James dunked his head under the water.

He looked at it. Looked at the house.

He came back up.

"Wow," he said. "This is a house."

"It really is."

They stared at each other, James in the water, Amelia at the edge of the green canoe. Something passed between them. Unspoken. Something like *be careful.* But like they both said it to each other. As in be careful now, yes, but let's be careful in everything that follows, too.

James took a deep breath.

And went under.

9

Murky, James thought, swimming head down, his hair floating above his head like short seaweed. He couldn't see much, not yet. Just the roof that seemed to vanish at the edges, drift off into the darkness of the deep.

He swam to it.

Far above him, in a place he could not see, a cloud moved from in front of the sun and some light crested the lake, warming Amelia, and revealing, for James, a piece of the house itself. Not quite like curtains parting, but as if a magician's naked hand pulled aside to show him a window it'd been hiding.

James looked down to the glass and felt the vertigo of being high up, like looking down into the courtyard of the mall, or the pause at the top of the Demon Drop at Cedar Point. How big was the house? How many stories?

He swam toward the glass. More details emerged.

Siding. Brick. A windowsill.

The flashlight was tied to the elastic band of his swim trunks. Treading by the side of the house, then planting his toes to the bricks for support, he untied the flashlight and brought it to the glass. He pressed his nose to the window.

Space, he thought. As if the word counted for many other words. *Room. Bedroom. The Unknown.*

It was much too dark to see anything and really the flashlight just reflected hard off the glass, becoming a second glowing circle on the window.

He pushed off and swam deeper.

Another window, a story lower than the first.

Two stories. A two-story home at the bottom of the lake.

He looked up, hoping to see Amelia's face through the surface. But it was all an unintelligible impression up there. Strong solid colors rippling. For a moment it looked like he *could* see her, could see someone, a giant's head, a head as large as the surface of the lake, peering down into the water at him. Then the impressions faded out at the edges, and James couldn't make out anything up top.

Without knowing it was coming, he reached the bottom of the lake and felt his feet sink into thick, soft mud. He was standing next to the house, impossible as it sounded. He reached out, into the darkness, into the murk, and flattened his hand against the bricks.

It was real. There was no doubting that.

A rush of cold water passed over his back, hugged him, nudged his fingertips off the bricks and onto glass.

Another window. A first floor window. James shined his light at it.

Blackness. Couldn't see a thing in there.

He had a sudden vision of someone talking to Amelia up top. Telling her they had to leave. Explaining the house, cracking the mystery, flattening the mystery whole.

A maritime police officer, perhaps. A fisherman.

What do you mean you were curious, miss? What is there to be curious about? There's a two-story home at the bottom of every lake in the United States! GET OUT OF HERE!

But there wasn't a two-story home at the bottom of every lake. As much as the idea suddenly comforted him.

He cupped his hands and pressed them against the glass.

Nothing. Couldn't make anything out. Looked like the possible outlines of furniture. But that was impossible.

Right?

Beginning to feel the tightness of holding his breath for too long, James shined his light up, taking in, for the first time, the full scope of the house.

A big one. Bigger than James had ever lived in.

Suddenly, he imagined Amelia laying in a bed in a second story bedroom. He imagined swimming up to the glass, treading outside, knocking on the glass, waking her.

Let me in?

Then he thought of waterlogged mattresses. Fabric about to burst with fish bones and muck.

He shined his light to the left of him and saw the edge of the house and knew that, if there was a front door— *of course there's a front door, it's a HOUSE, James*—it was around that corner.

His lungs told him to get up top. Go see Amelia.

Instead, he walked, astronaut-like, toward the brick edge of the house.

A thought occurred to him, natural as it was: if the front door was open, why not step inside?

At the corner of the house (*the house!*) he looked over his shoulder, into the blackness, the rest of the lake.

There was no sense of being watched, not exactly, it was something much less focused than that. As if all that blackness was one dumb eye, pointed in his direction, capable of simply observing the small teenaged boy at the base of the house, with no brain to transmit the news to.

Not watched. But seen.

James took the turn, shining his light ahead, and saw another window. A front window. A simple thing anybody would see if they were pulling up to the front of the house in a car.

His chest constricted, his head starting to throb, James continued past a garden of seaweed below the windowsill. The mud was getting softer and he trained the light at his feet. The shadows of the fluttering seaweed fooled him into thinking he saw fingers draw back into the folds.

Then James stepped on something much harder than the lake's mushy bottom.

It was a single stone step. Maybe more of them were buried.

He looked up.

James was looking at the front door of the house.

He gasped, if such a thing can be done underwater, and the bubble that escaped his throat was perhaps the last one he had left.

It wasn't a full front door. It was *half* of one; the left half, still hinged, swaying in unseen waves, pulses Amelia couldn't feel above. There was no right half of the door and James thought it looked like the wood had been intentionally replaced with darkness.

Come, it all seemed to say, the left half swaying. *Come in.*

He made to move, made to come in.

Then stopped.

He needed to breathe. Needed to breathe *now*.

Using the mossy, slick step as a springboard, he bent at the knees and sprang up.

As he cut through the water he had a terrible vision of himself dying on the way up; a corpse by the time he broke the surface, Amelia screaming as a decayed and flaking James bobbed in the water less than two feet from the green canoe.

He closed his eyes. Almost *felt* the change occurring; life to death. Dying while moving. The quick wrinkling of his skin. The shrinking of his lungs, his bladder, his heart.

Then he actually did feel something.

Something like thick noodles along the full side of his body, from his chest to his toes. Something like hair.

Still rising, James opened his eyes and saw he was passing the dark square of an upper story window, just as a new cloud covered the sun again, and any more visibility was taken.

When he broke the surface he breathed huge, and saw the canoe was much farther from him than he thought it would be.

Amelia was sitting in the middle of it, staring at him without speaking. A figurine, James thought, fashioned to look desperately investigative.

"We need scuba gear," James called, swimming toward her.

"What?"

"Scuba gear. We need to take lessons."

"Why?"

"Because we're going back down there," James said. "And we're gonna wanna stay down there longer than we can hold our breath."

"We are?"

"The front door is open. Half a door. Hard to explain." He reached the canoe and held tight to the ladder. He was breathing hard. "It's a little freaky," he said. "But man ... it's awesome."

Amelia felt a chill.

The front door is open.

James climbed the ladder.

"Go on," he said. He unhooked the flashlight from his waist and tossed it to her. "See for yourself."

10

Half a front door. Hard to explain.

But that pretty much explained it.

Amelia didn't like being down here one bit. Didn't like the world of open black behind her (*like a bloated, gibbering madman planted the house to draw you and James in, a carrot for the teenage donkeys, a madman that's gonna suddenly explode from that darkness, his slobber floating up to gather about the canoe, as he grips you by the hair and drags you inside his house, HIS house, Amelia*), didn't like the open half of the door, the way she could swim right in with no resistance at all.

It was impossible not to imagine something living inside: a watery creature, undiscovered, unlisted, nesting.

This is insane, she thought.

But wasn't it fun, too? Wasn't it also the most thrilling thing she'd ever seen?

Knowing her time below was short, she'd swam straight for the front door James had told her about. She didn't stop at any windows, didn't try to look inside. So, standing on the stone step, handrails (*handrails!*) on either side of the small stone porch, she had more air to spare than James did when he arrived at the same spot.

Shining the light along the four rectangular sides of the half door, as though to somehow symbolically create a passage *through* light, Amelia did not hesitate to enter the house. Scared or not, this *was* thrilling.

By her bare toes she sprang up from the stone step and swam into the house.

Using her arms in a kind of breaststroke, the flashlight showed her the doorframe, then a piece of a wall, then nothing, as the light was behind her. She thought for a moment that it was no different than entering an abandoned house on the side of Chauncey Road. She'd done that once with a good friend named Marla. Together they took photos, believing they were capturing the truest essence of living and life.

Emptiness.

But when she brought her arms forward again, with a mind to propel herself deeper into the house, the light showed her something that caused her to do something she'd never done before in her life.

Amelia screamed underwater.

It was a coatrack, nothing more, and there wasn't even a coat hanging to make her think she'd seen a person. And yet ...

It didn't belong here, she knew. Certainly didn't belong here the way it was, standing, erect, as though ignorant of the thousands of pounds of water and waves enveloping it.

It's not bobbing, she thought, shining the light to the floor where the base of the coatrack was firmly flat to the wooden boards. *It's not bobbing or floating or even leaning.*

She was in a foyer, this much was clear. Beside the coatrack was a small table, the place someone would perhaps place their keys when they returned from town.

There was even a glass bowl on the table. The exact place for keys, Amelia thought.

Her lungs felt tight from the lack of air.

Why isn't the bowl floating? She wanted to know. *Why isn't everything?*

She shined the light behind her, to the half door, absurdly frightened of seeing a face there, the homeowner, a man in an overcoat perhaps, standing on the mossy front step.

Who let you in?

She swam a foot deeper into the foyer, saw the table wasn't so small after all. It was more of a credenza; a gorgeous piece of Victorian woodwork that didn't look waterlogged, didn't look bad at all for being at the bottom of a lake. In fact, Amelia believed it looked usable, as she ran her fingers along its surface, then the rim of the glass bowl.

Because she had expected to find nothing in this house, nothing but fish and rotten wood, the reality of touching the glass confused her. In a way, the contact removed any veil of magic.

This is impossible, she thought. *All of this. IMPOSSIBLE.*

She looked to the ceiling, expecting to see clutter above, small rocks or dead fish obeying the laws of physics, flat to the plaster.

But the ceiling was bare.

But *not* bare.

A light bulb.

She shined her own light ahead. A hallway. From the foyer to the rest of the house.

Despite the fact that she needed to breathe, soon, Amelia crossed the foyer. Her mostly naked body was very cold, and getting colder the deeper she traveled into the house. But she badly wanted to see one more thing before leaving. One more piece of verification before she swam up to the canoe.

Before she reached any larger room, her light showed her a mirror on the hall wall.

Don't look into it.

It was the first thought that came to mind. Just like when she'd told herself not to look in the mirror at home when she had a feeling she looked like shit.

Just like it, but not just like.

Don't look into it.

Of course the space (*the whole house, the lake, too*) surrounding her beam of light was a blackness as dark as burial. And the objects that were revealed, in the beam, rippled, unnaturally. Yes, an underwater mirror in a pitch-black house might have been a bad idea.

But Amelia couldn't resist.

Bubbles erupted from between her lips as she gasped, mutely, catching sight of her face in the glass.

Medusa.

But not Medusa. Just *Amelia*. Not a wrinkled gray Gorgon who turned you to stone, but rather a distorted representation of a young woman, her skin as pale as the drapes in a morgue, her hair floating like seaweed (*snakes*) above her frightened, but curious face. It was such an everyday task, looking in the mirror, that she'd instinctively expected to see her everyday face. But this woman, this *her*, this Amelia had rippling skin, cheeks half an inch higher than they normally were. Lips curled up at their ends in a false smile.

Even her eyes looked different. Unfocused. As if Amelia were privy to the one sight no person truly wanted to see; this is what she might look like dead.

Found dead.

One day.

Found drowned.

Drowned.

Amelia needed to get back to the top. Needed to get air.

She shined the light once more, deeper into the house. A pair of matching bubbles escaped her nostrils.

Then she swam from the mirror, back to the foyer, toward the half front door.

You're not gonna make it and James is gonna call the police and they're gonna find you floating down here. Or maybe not floating … maybe they'll find you flat on the floor, like that coatrack, disobeying the laws of a lake.

She crossed the threshold and tried not to think about what it would feel like; drowning. Was this it? The earliest stages? The last few moments before a person understood there would be no getting back up?

Would she see stars first? Would she black out before or after the pain of it became unbearable?

James. Swim toward James.

Amelia exited the house and foolishly thought about turning back, to close the door, as if she'd been rude for leaving it open. But there was no door to close and her arms and legs were already propelling her up. Up.

Up?

She couldn't see the surface above and for one insane second she thought maybe she was swimming down.

She was starting to believe she was going to die.

Curiosity killed the cat and *the snooping seventeen-year-old girl.*

James would mistake her floating body for a living one. He'd think she was joking.

First dates. And whom would he tell about *this* date? Just as he'd told Amelia about the girl who broke her arm bowling, who would hear about the girl that went diving and popped out of the water as a bloated, veined corpse?

But death hadn't happened yet.

No blackout. No stars.

She swam harder, pulling herself up, as if the water had rungs of its own.

The last thing she saw before breaking the surface was the second story window, partially shadowed by the roof.

Is there a dresser up there? She wondered, absurdly, too close to passing out. *A nightstand and a wardrobe, too?*

Then she broke the surface and all her terrible imaginings dissipated into the air she desperately breathed.

Part horror, part triumph, the sound echoed across the third lake and chilled James cold.

"Hey!" he called, gripping the canoe's side. "Holy shit! Are you okay?"

Amelia wiped snot from her nose and lips.

"We need scuba gear," she said.

"Yeah, that's what I—"

"It's furnished, James."

They locked eyes. James in the canoe. Amelia treading water four feet from the ladder.

"It's what?"

"It's furnished."

11

Amelia didn't recognize how claustrophobic the third lake made her feel until they set out to leave it. Then the word struck her like a slap.

Claustrophobic.

She was afraid the canoe wouldn't squeeze out the way it squeezed in. Afraid they'd be stuck there, on the third lake, with the house, forever.

It was silly, of course. They could just swim through the tunnel, could walk on shore, a dozen different ways to leave. But still, she'd felt it.

Panic.

But the canoe made it out just the way it'd come in. Only now there were even more paint flakes in the water, more of a dent in the canoe.

"Uncle Bob's got a good long hose," James said, as they reached shore at last; the short stretch of sand that constituted Uncle Bob's little beach.

"We keep coming back to hoses," Amelia said.

"We do. I guess that's our spirit animal?"

But Amelia thought of the dead fish floating a foot below the surface of the third lake.

James got out of the canoe.

"It won't work," Amelia said. "The hose."

"It won't?"

"No. I tried it before. It doesn't work like a straw."

James looked thoughtful. He looked out across the first lake but Amelia knew he was actually looking farther than that.

"Does your uncle have scuba gear?"

"He might."

"Would you know how to use it?"

"No." He looked ponderous again. "My cousin has diving gear."

"That's good."

"Yeah. I'll get it from him tonight."

Clipped syllables. Short sentences. Amelia knew why.

They were planning on returning to the third lake.

Without discussing the idea, they were going back.

This meant something.

"Tomorrow then," James said.

"Yes. Wait ... no. I work tomorrow."

"What time?"

"During the day."

"Where do you work?"

"Darlene's Grocery."

"You do?"

"Yeah."

"Cool."

"Yeah."

"All right."

"The next day," Amelia said.

James nodded.

"All right."

They looked into each other's eyes. Something quiet passed. They'd been given a teaser, a foyer, a hall with a mirror, and they wanted to see more.

You'd go back with or without her, James thought. But the idea felt ugly.

They nodded at the same time, both pretending they were agreeing to a second date in two days. But really both were saying yes, yes I'd go back alone.

I'd go back this second if I could.

12

Darlene's Grocery featured twelve aisles of everything a family could need. *From food to toilet paper,* Amelia's coworker Marcy liked to say. *We've got both ends covered.* And it was true. All ends, in fact. Including the flippers and snorkels and masks that made up the small, but popular, water aisle.

Working the next day's shift, Amelia passed those bathing suits and water-wings and thought about the house countless times.

What is it?

Specifically she thought about the coatrack and the glass bowl, neither of which should have stayed put in an environment like that. And the more she thought about it, the more the pristine state of the wood walls bothered her, too, the more the string hanging straight down from the light bulb in the foyer confused her.

What is it?

These three words made a bigger racket than the more obvious four:

Why is it there?

She stocked shelves with paper towels and cereal and helped Marcy void an order. She talked briefly to the delivery guys from Saxon Foods about the apples and why some of them were bad and one of them asked her if she could do him a favor and keep quiet about the state of the apples? They were fine when they left Saxon, he said. He must've gone too fast over a bump. Boss would be angry. Amelia inspected the apples, found they were good enough, and told him it would be their little secret.

Our little secret.

But no fully furnished house at the bottom of a lake was anybody's little secret. *Somebody* had to know about it.

Who?

She bagged groceries, careful with the eggs, and made small talk with the regulars. She passed the mirror in the employee hall twice and both times noted the fixed detail of herself in the glass. She swept aisles. She aligned the labels on the soup cans so the customers could read the flavors. And yet, despite all these distractions, *somebody* had to know about the house.

It almost made her feel like she was being watched. Watched at work. Spies in the parking lot outside Darlene's waiting to ask her if she touched anything down there, prepared to search her car for wet spots.

Watched. But not quite watched. More like *seen*.

Uncle Bob?

Did he know about it? Amelia thought he had to. How could you own a home on the first lake and never think to check out the graffitied tunnel on the second? Never pass over the house James and Amelia had seen on their *very first* turn in the canoe?

It was covered up, Amelia reminded herself. Yes, the brush. Kinda made it hard to see the tunnel. The bright graffiti. The drawings of dicks and tits.

She wanted to ask Bob herself. Maybe James already had. Standing alone at register two she checked her phone for any texts. There were none.

No *Bob knows* or *Bob says it's a movie set* or anything from James at all.

So … *had* James talked to his uncle about it? And why did that idea make her feel so … *bad* inside?

What is it?

Marcy finished bagging a customer's meats at register one and continued the 'perpetual conversation,' the way some coworkers have of picking up a story exactly where they left off, even if that was two days past.

"So *Tommy* thinks it's safe," she said. Then she winked.

Amelia wasn't sure who Tommy was or what was safe. She winked back.

She thought of the house.

In her mind's eye the half door was swinging smoothly on unseen waves. In her vision, the sun must have been directly above the lake because Amelia saw details in the wood of that door she hadn't seen yesterday in person. And through the dark open half, she imagined a friendly face, barely distinguishable, perhaps her own reflection distorted in the hall mirror, and a voice, too.

Come back anytime, Amelia. Annnnnnyyyyy tiiiiiimmmmmmeeeeee.

"Oh boy," Marcy said, half a finger jammed up her nose, another pointing to the front doors.

Amelia looked up.

"James?"

It was James. Walking toward the registers. And he was carrying something straight out of a science fiction movie set. Or maybe something from the bottom of a fish tank.

"Hi," he said. "Sorry to stalk you."

"I'm glad you're here."

Relief. Together again. As if his presence alone denoted they were already on their way back to the third lake.

"Look," he said, half lifting the monstrosity in his arms.

"Scuba," Amelia said.

But it wasn't scuba. It was an enormous moon helmet and the gold breathing tube that went with it.

"My cousin's," James said.

"Did you tell him what you needed it for?"

They exchanged a glance then, a knowing one. Amelia may as well have asked, *did you tell ANYBODY about it?*

"No. I just told him I wanted to go diving."

He hadn't told anybody about the house, Amelia could tell. She felt a second wave of relief. This one was peppered with a little shame. A little self-examination. But why not keep something to yourself?

Why not keep a secret?

"Uncle Bob knew about the third lake," James said.

"Good"

"Good?"

"I mean ... like ... of course he knows. Right?"

"Right. But he said he never goes out there. I didn't tell him we did. I just told him it looked like there might be a third lake. He said it's more of a swamp. Said it's ugly."

"Ugly," Amelia repeated.

"What's the scuba gear for?" Marcy asked, stepping out from behind register 1.

"Never mind," James said.

"Never mind," Amelia said.

Marcy looked from one to the other.

"Are the two of you ... weird or something?"

James smiled at Amelia and carried the gear back toward the glass front doors. Before exiting he stopped and turned to face her.

"We're doing this," he mouthed, silently.

Amelia whispered, *"Yes."*

"You guys *are* weird," Marcy said.

Amelia's smile fell slowly from her face as James exited. Not because she wasn't happy. Not because she wasn't excited that he'd gone out and got the suit. But because, already, the house seemed to require a more careful consideration than any simple smile could supply.

We're doing this, yes, Amelia thought. *But ... what is it?*

13

It wasn't just the helmet and breathing tube that were gold; the *whole* suit shimmered.

That night they tried it on in James's backyard. His parents were asleep inside and so they had to be quiet. They tried. But they laughed, stumbled, and felt like the first men on the moon. Acted like them, too, pretending to place flags on the moon's surface, jamming actual sticks in the dirt. It was awkward, it was thrilling, it was frightening.

"One rule," Amelia said as James removed the helmet, exposing his young face in the porch light surrounded by bugs.

"Only one?"

"No *hows* or *whys*."

"What?"

"We don't ask how the house ended up there and we don't ask why it's furnished. We don't ask how or why it works."

James understood.

"No *hows* or *whys*," he agreed.

James stuck out one gold gloved mitt and Amelia, smiling, shook it.

With that contact, both felt the full thrilling power of their discovery.

A clubhouse. If they wanted it to be.

And it wasn't just the house. No. It was the fourth lake they were swimming in, too.

For the first time in either of their lives, they were falling in love.

14

Alone underwater. Alone in the house.

Breathing.

Two minutes in, James felt his pulse quickening and thought he better get up to the surface before it was too late. But he was wearing the helmet and he didn't need to go up like he'd had to two days ago. He could spend more than an hour down here if he wanted to.

The breathing tube led out the front door and up to the canoe. There it was connected to a compressor that Amelia watched when she wasn't staring into the water, staring at the roof of the house.

James was no longer thinking about speedboats and screaming girls in bikinis. Amelia *had* to be impressed by all this.

You're in a house underwater and all you can think about is Amelia.

It was true and so he laughed and the laughter splattered against the glass dome protecting him.

He stood in the foyer, shining the flashlight down the hall where Amelia had looked at herself in the mirror. He could see the glass of it, hanging on the left wall. And beyond it, a much larger room, the dimensions of which he could only begin to ascertain.

As he stepped toward it, the breathing tube snagged on the half-front door and the tug was as slight as a tap on the shoulder.

The suit was bulky and the gloves made ape hands of his fingers and he couldn't turn as quickly as he wanted to. He felt too slow and too blocky. With his free hand he gave the hose a twirl, sent a ripple through it, hoping it would come loose from whatever snag was stopping him from going farther into the house.

It worked.

Free, he looked into the mirror as he passed it, smiling behind the glass helmet.

It was the visage, James thought, of young love.

He saw a room ahead, piecemeal, made up of the brief patches of light he afforded it. It was a dining room. The table and chairs told him *that*. But nothing told him how the table and chairs remained fixed as they were to the floor.

Nor did anything explain the rug beneath the legs of the chairs. Or the hundreds of trinkets that lined the shelves of a glass cabinet against the right wall.

No hows, James thought. *No whys.*

It was impossible not to feel like he'd broken into this home. If not for the darkness, the distortion, and the cold, James would have counted himself lucky for not having run into whoever owned it.

He moon-stepped toward the dining room and got snagged again.

"Dammit."

He turned and sent another ripple through the tube. It traveled the length of the hose, slow motion, vanishing through the dark rectangle of the half front door, into the muddy front yard beyond.

Then, the ripple came back.

Toward him.

As if James was outside the house and the hose was here, snagged where he stood.

James trained the flashlight on the front door, tracing the rectangular doorframe. Mud motes and minnows passed through his light, then vanished fast into the darkness

He waited for a second tug from outside of the house. Another ripple.

You're breathing too hard, man.

But that wasn't possible. Unless someone sent it his way.

He thought of Amelia up top.

Had she sent him the wave in the breathing tube? She must have. But was she trying to tell him something?

Someone's up there, he thought. *Someone telling her to get her boyfriend out of the water and get home. NOW.*

James lumbered back to the front door. Peering over the threshold he saw the tube was indeed snagged on one of the porch handrails.

He took the hose between a gloved finger and thumb.

Did you just call yourself her boyfriend?

The hose came loose from the handrail and James easily coiled the slack. He re-entered the house.

He wanted to go deeper this time. Deeper into the house. Deeper into the lake.

Deeper in love.

Is *this love? Is that happening?*

He got to the dining room quickly, more agile than he was moments ago. And despite the darkness ahead, the darkness everywhere, he felt safe.

Alive.

He floated to the dining room table.

The flashlight showed him a tablecloth, serving dishes, folded napkins, and eight high-backed chairs. A chandelier hung from the ceiling, swaying gently with the unseen waves alive here at the bottom of the lake.

There were paintings on the walls. Landscapes that seemed to undulate, as if something lived beneath the yellow grass.

How?

Unlit candles. Sconces. Utensils. All of it sedentary on the table. On shelves. On plates.

How?

A solid wood buffet. A tray upon it. Not floating. Not moving at all.

HOW?

"No hows," James said into the helmet. "No whys."

Amelia was far above him. Watching the compressor.

James went deeper.

The hose followed smoothly. The hose did not get snagged.

And James went deeper into the house.

15

Past the dining room, a study. One wall lined with books.

Intact. Bound. Underwater.

Books.

James trained the flashlight on the titles. Foreign languages, or maybe the letters had been ruined by water after all, stolen a piece at a time, the three lines that made up an A, the three of an F. By the bookshelf was a chair, solidly planted on the ground, beside it an end table with an ashtray, beyond it a bay window. By James's light, the world outside the glass was pitch black, yet he could see *something* out there. Seaweed waving at the base of the window, mud floating on submerged waves, the pulse of the lake.

James sat down in the study chair. Put his gloved hands on the armrests.

He noted the wallpaper, tiny ducks fleeing a shadow-faced hunter.

A stepladder to reach the higher books.

A second door, behind the study chair.

James grew colder. Physically, yes, but in a fearful way, too. Scary thought, himself seated in the study of an impossible home at the bottom of a lake. It suddenly felt possible, no, *likely*, that something dead could come floating through the door he'd entered by. Something falling to pieces, pulling apart, coming toward him, consciously or not, a drifting once-was, unglued.

He tried to pick up the ashtray on the end table. It wouldn't move.

James stared at it for a long time, resisting the word *why?*

He got up and adjusted the tube's slack, giving him another twenty feet of walking room.

Astronaut-like, he rounded the chair and opened the second door. Because he didn't have the flashlight lifted yet, wasn't pointing it ahead, he saw nothing. In that moment, that single drumbeat of absolute darkness, he felt as if he was stepping into the nothingness of death, a real end, a place where he'd never be able to find Amelia, never find warmth, solace, confidence, triumph, reason, or love ever again.

Don't enter this room.

A dark thought to have at a dark threshold.

But James entered the room.

He brought the flashlight up and yelled, two involuntary syllables crashing against the helmet's glass.

A pale face in the flashlight. Staring into his eyes.

James stepped back, knocking his elbow against the wall.

But it was only a painting.

"Jesus," James said. Then he laughed at himself. And he wished Amelia had been here to hear him scream.

Not a face. Not eyes after all. Two plums on a white table, the edge of the table like a perfectly set, unsmiling mouth.

A rippling still life beneath the (*roof*) waves.

James leaned toward the painting, bringing the helmet's glass half an inch from the canvas. He thought it was an oil painting. He recalled the cliché *like oil and water.* He wondered if that had something to do with why it was still intact.

He shined the flashlight around the room, getting details the way he got anything in this house; in pieces. As if a puzzle had been dropped into the third lake many years ago, and now James and Amelia were here to put it back together again.

A brown leather couch. A long, thin window. Cabinet doors. A coffee table. A rug.

"A rug," James said. He knelt to the ground and ran a glove over the hundreds of tiny tendrils, red and white fabric sea anemones.

It occurred to James that he was in a *nice* house. The nicest he'd ever been in.

He rose and turned and saw a pool table. The balls were racked at one end. The cue waited at the other.

Play me, it seemed to say. *But don't ask how.*

James gripped a stick from a wall mount. Then he paused.

Staring into the space beyond the other end of the table it felt like someone could be there. Someone to play a game with. As if, were he to break the balls, unseen fingers might take the stick from him, might go next.

He set the cue back into the mount. Then, taking the breathing tube's slack up by his hip, he exited the lounge.

He stepped into a new room, but before he could determine what sort it was, his flashlight died.

Darkness.

Alone with it.

Clumsily, through the ape gloves, James clicked the flashlight's switch on/off, on/off. He shook it, then cracked it against his hip. The suit was too bulky there so he tried it against his other arm. Too bulky there, too. He raised it up to his helmet, brought the dead flashlight back and ... stopped.

Don't break your helmet, man. What are you thinking?

He let his arms fall by his sides. No light.

He stared into the darkness ahead, felt the cold of the darkness behind. Without light, he could be anywhere in the house. Upstairs, downstairs. Outside. In. The house might not exist at all. Why, he could be standing on the bottom of an empty lake. Could be sleeping. Could be awake.

James tried to smile, tried to stay calm, but it was very hard to do in the dark.

"Hi, Amelia," he said, thinking a pretend-communication with her might help. It didn't. And he wished he hadn't. It made him feel more alone. Made her seem further away. Or like he was leaving her name down here.

Like he was delivering Amelia's name to the darkness.

He tried the flashlight again.

On/off.

It worked.

Light.

Ahead, not twenty feet from where he stood rooted, was a staircase. A wide one. Two could walk it, side by side.

Amelia, he thought. *The light didn't work for a second and man I thought I was gonna shit the suit.*

A red and white runner lined the stairs, molded to each step.

James held the light fixed at the top for a long time.

He wanted to climb the stairs, wanted to see what the second floor had to offer. But he'd had enough. For now.

He exited the way he'd come, not pausing to examine a single item. Through the lounge, the study, the dining room, the foyer, and the half-front door.

Swimming up, he felt bulkier than ever. The house seemed to sink in slow motion beside him. And when he broke the surface, Amelia's smiling face was as welcome as any he'd ever seen.

James bobbed for a moment, treading six feet from the canoe.

Amelia called out.

"How'd it go?"

Back in the canoe, he told her. And with each detail, her wonder grew wider.

"So you made it to the bottom of the stairs?" she asked.

"Yes."

"So I should probably climb them."

James paused before answering.

"Sure. If you want to."

"In the name of exploring," Amelia said, "I need to go further than you did, right?"

"Sure. Yes."

Amelia clapped her hands together.

"Help me get the helmet on."

"The flashlight was acting up on me," he said.

"It was?"

"Yeah."

Amelia took it from him and tried it out.

"It's working now."

"Yeah. But, you know, it went out for a minute."

Amelia looked over the edge, to the roof in the murky shadows.

"If it goes out," she said, "I'll just feel my way back."

James laughed. He tried to recall exactly how scared he'd been, but now that he was safe, it was hard.

"Are you sure?"

"Yes."

While she got into the suit, she thought about being in the dark down there alone. She repeated phrases like *it's worth it* and *nobody ever did anything great by being too scared to do it.*

These helped.

Before she slipped her arms into the sleeves, James reached out and touched her arm.

"What did you do that for?"

But the look in James's eyes told her that he didn't quite know. That he'd seen her pale soft skin and had wanted to touch her. And that was all it was.

"Sorry," he said. He could feel himself turning red.

"Don't be," Amelia said. She considered foolishly reaching out and touching him, too. To make him feel better. And because she wanted to.

Then she slipped her arms into the sleeves. Her hands into the huge gold gloves.

Once she got in the water, James tapped on the helmet's glass.

She looked up at him, breathing steady, inquisitive. James thought she looked like a kid, a small girl in that big suit.

"Careful of the hose," James said. "It could get snagged on something. Doorways. Tables."

Amelia gave him a gloved thumbs-up.

Then she went under.

James watched her sinking past the roof, into the shadows. Soon she was only a tube, a thin line swallowed by the darkness.

Then James saw an eye, looking at him from the upstairs window.

"Amelia!" he yelled. He went to grab the hose, to yank on it, to pull her back up. But the eye moved and James saw it was a fish.

Only a fish in the upstairs window. As natural as anything could be in a lake.

Only a fish.

16

The flashlight was acting up on me.

Amelia stood at the bottom of the staircase, shining the flashlight in question up to the top of the stairs.

Maybe she should've heeded James's warning. Maybe they should have gone and bought another one.

But she'd wanted to look adventurous. And she was *feeling* adventurous. And when she was still up on the sunny surface it didn't sound so bad if the lights went out below. Dark and cold. It was just underwater, after all. What was dark but the absence of light? And what was cold but a temperature? Night in winter. Amelia had experienced it all before.

Still ...

She was kneeling, studying the runner that lined the stairs. The hose's slack was delicately piled beside her. She didn't know the first thing about water damage or what ought to happen to a rug that's been underwater for this long, but she could guess that it shouldn't look as fine as it did.

It looked new.

Kind of.

In a classic sort of way.

She looked to the top of the stairs, the light still focused on the highest step. It was black up there. Impenetrable. No light came through a second story window. Probably blocked by the roof. Or maybe all the doors were closed up there.

All the doors.

"Here we go," Amelia said, talking to James just like he talked to her. No actual communication between them.

She got up and used the bannister to balance herself.

The flashlight was acting up on me.

It didn't sound so shameful now, so unadventurous to go and get a better light. The square at the top of the stairs, the gateway to the second story, reminded Amelia of the sort of hole you chance upon in a forest floor, then step widely around it.

Amelia took the first stair up. Then the next.

Quick now, she was halfway there and thinking how James hadn't been this far, how maybe nobody had been this far in the whole wide world.

She moon-stepped the next stair. Then the next.

Ahead, the light didn't reveal much more than the beginning of a hallway.

"Well, James, here we are. Dating. Is this our second date? No. This would probably be our third. Two dates underwater. One up above. Good for us. We're insane."

She took the next step.

"Some people go to the movies, some people make out in their cars, parked behind schools."

Another step.

"Some people meet for coffee. Some for drinks. Men and women meet for drinks. Happens all the time."

Another.

"But us? We're taking turns in a crazy place."

She liked that. *Taking turns in a crazy place.* Sounded like ... like love.

Two steps from the top and she stopped.

Far ahead the light showed her a door.

"It'd be a bad time for the flashlight to break," she said.

A single door. At the end of a long wood paneled hallway. Floating between her and the door were a few fish. All of them dead.

"They swim on their sides," she pretended to tell James. "That's all. Side-swimmers."

Darkness and cold water split by the beam.

She understood that she wished she had less slack. She understood, clearly, that she'd like a reason to turn back.

"No," she said, shaking her head inside the helmet. "Let's explore."

The fear ebbed, leaving only the adrenaline of exploration to play with.

Amelia began walking, plodding, astronaut-esque, toward the door at the end of the hall in the house at the bottom of a lake.

17

No doors along the hall and it started to feel as though Amelia was being shuffled toward the only door, the one at the far end. Felt like a gentle but wide wave was nudging her, from behind, guiding her there.

She bounded, slowly, past mirrors, looking just long enough to see the various expressions on her face behind the bubble helmet. The flashlight reflected harsh off the glass, the water distorted things, and Amelia hardly recognized herself at all.

The door was arched at the top, the kind of door Amelia always wanted for her bedroom as a child. It looked partially functional and partially pure fiction. The sort of door that asked a person to open it.

Amelia put a gloved hand on the doorknob and the door moved with no more movement than that.

"James," she said. "You want to take it from here?"

She didn't want to think these words. She wanted to say them. Because nobody would speak out loud if they were scared. If Amelia was *scared* she wouldn't want to make a sound, wouldn't want to attract a mother fish or a who-knows-what buried on the second story of a house at the bottom of a lake. If Amelia was *scared* she wouldn't walk with such confidence. She'd worry about the breathing tube, about the pressure inside the helmet. She'd be sweating, trembling, too clumsy to guide the hose alongside her. She'd be crying, retreating, curling up into a ball, sitting down wherever she was, floating, letting the water take her. If Amelia was scared she wouldn't have climbed the steps, wouldn't be standing at an impossible (*and open*) door that should have disintegrated a long time ago.

She swallowed once, hard, and thought she could hear its echo, the whole lake swallowing with her.

A movement, subtle, but everywhere.

A breath.

Amelia crossed the threshold and entered the room upstairs.

"Oh!"

A yellow dress, floated across the room toward her. Floating horizontal, it looked as though someone were wearing it.

Seven feet above the floor.

Amelia ducked. It was a silly thing to do, as the yellow dress rode an unseen current and rose to the ceiling.

When you opened the door, you caused a wave—

"Say the words out loud!" she demanded of herself. "You're *not* scared!"

The dress folded in on itself and rose to the ceiling in a corner of the room.

Amelia stepped farther into the room and kept the beam on the dress, studying its yellow fabric, the tiny frills at the shoulder ends. She could imagine the creamy, pale skin those frills once laid upon, could imagine the form of a pretty woman filling the dress, before the woman took it off and released it ... letting it float from her fingertips, deeper into the dark room.

Amelia felt the presence of something to her right and turned fast.

She brought a hand to her mouth to stifle a gasp but her fingers clunked against the glass and she stared at a second dress, a red one, floating, too, but as if standing up, as if on a hanger, suspended, perfectly upright.

Amelia stepped back and found herself against the door.

It was closed now.

How?

"No hows!"

But her voice was small, so small in the glass helmet.

In the beam, it looked like the red dress could take a step toward her if it wanted to, could approach her, quicker than she herself could move.

Then the water took it, folding it at the waist.

Behind it, an open wardrobe was revealed.

Empty wooden hangers within.

Slowly, Amelia went to it. She fingered the hangers, her gloved hands too clumsy to do anything but fumble.

She trained the light up and saw a gray dress flat to the ceiling. If a woman *were* inside it, that woman would be facing her.

To her left a mauve dress floated toward her, level enough to look occupied, as if someone were limping in it, drunk perhaps, the water filling the fabric in such a way to make it look curvy, embodied, in use, worn by somebody who was not quite right, somebody who was ...

"Deformed," Amelia said. Because she didn't want to just think it.

When the dress reached her, Amelia held out her gloved hands and the fabric folded limply over them. Gently, she let it fall away and saw behind it a fourth dress.

This one was black, positioned near the floor, as if sitting up, watching Amelia directly.

Amelia shined the light everywhere. She counted three more dresses. Floating in the corners, where the floors met the walls and the walls met each other, too.

At either side of the room she saw sets of twin doors, doors that should, if Amelia had her bearings, lead eventually back toward the staircase. She understood that there must be bedrooms through these doors, other rooms, rooms with windows, at least one of which she and James had seen from the canoe.

She stepped toward the doors to her right, to the side of the house James floated above.

She reached for the doors, saw they were open, and pressed a bulky gold palm against them.

A blue dress emerged from the opened space and floated over her helmet, into the darkness behind her.

She tracked it with the flashlight, back across the room, where it sank, momentarily, to the floor, at the hem of the black dress.

"Not scared," she said.

Breathing deeply, she passed through the twin open doors.

18

"Wow," Amelia said, the helmet only half off. "Wow wow wow wow *wow!*"

She grabbed James by the face, the gloves wet on his cheeks.

"You went upstairs?" James asked.

"Went upstairs?! *Went upstairs?!* James! It's incredible. It's the most astonishing thing I've ever seen. There were dresses floating, beds with rippling sheets, vanities, and the closets ... oh my goodness *God* the closets."

Relieved to see her, and twice as glad to see her having so much fun, James started laughing.

"You're really excited!"

"Excited?! I can't even ... can't even find the words. This is ... this is ... it's ..."

"Miraculous," James said. Then he looked over the edge of the canoe to the roof. "Impossible."

"It's fabulous. It's magic. It's like the most important discovery ever made."

Amelia was hardly aware that she was standing in the canoe. James balanced it with every excited gesture she made.

"We have to tell people," she said. "We have to. How can we not?"

"Maybe we should."

"No!" Amelia said, her eyes wild with revelation. "We can't tell a *soul*. People will ruin it because that's what people do." She looked to the shore surrounding the third lake. "No. It's ours. For now. For as long as we want it, it's ours."

"Okay." James laughed. "I really need to check out the upstairs."

"Oh yes you do. Oh *yes* you do."

"How many rooms were up there?"

Amelia slipped out of the suit as she answered. James stared where the red fabric of her bikini bottom met her smooth skin.

"Seven? I think there are seven rooms up there. Three per side. And the center one. The dressing room. The powder room? I've never been in a room like it before. Dresses everywhere."

"Wow."

"Yes. *Wow.* I tried opening one of the windows. That one." She pointed below. "I tried to wave up to you, but the hose ... that was as far as it went."

"You maxed out the hose?"

"I did."

"Weren't you scared of it breaking?"

"I wasn't. I just didn't care. *James.* It's breathtaking. It's the most incredible thing I've ever ever *ever* seen."

She was out of the suit now. Her half naked body shone in the waning sun. James could count the droplets on her skin.

"Can't we just spend the night?" she asked.

"What?"

"No," she said, frowning. "I guess we can't. But man ... *that* would be amazing. To spend the night here. *Inside.* That's impossible, right?"

James laughed.

"You *really* had a good time in there."

"I did. I really did. I was scared. So scared. But I never felt unsafe. You know? What. A. Thrill."

James saw epiphany in her eyes. It thrilled him right back.

"James," she said, squatting in front of him. James tried not to look at her bikini bottom. "It's what I've been looking for my whole life. It's something so nonsensical that it makes fun of every sensible thing in the world. It's impossible. But it's here. Can we keep it?"

Can we keep it, James repeated in his mind. *As if we're dating. No longer just on a date. Now ... dating.*

"Yes," he said, smiling. "We can keep it. And we're going to keep it. And it's ours."

"Man," Amelia said.

She leaned forward and kissed him on the lips. Then her lips parted and James felt her delicate tongue snake upon his own.

When she pulled away from him, he was stunned speechless.

But Amelia was not.

"We need a second suit," she said. "We need to go down there together."

James nodded, as if breaking apart an unseen spell.

"We need to kiss again is what we need to do."

Amelia looked at his lips.

They kissed again.

"We need scuba," he said, when they pulled apart.

"Yes. Two suits. Should we take classes?"

They made plans to take lessons. They baked in the sun. They swam above the house. They paddled home.

They talked the entire way, all about the house. It was impossible to bring up anything else. Uncle Bob was waiting for them on shore, his bare feet on the small sandy beach.

"What did you two do to my canoe?" he asked, staring at the chipped paint, the dents, the crazy diving suit between the benches.

James and Amelia looked quick to one another. James opened his mouth to lie but Bob held up an open palm.

"It doesn't matter. You have no idea how many objects I broke before I turned twenty. You guys went diving?"

"Yeah."

Uncle Bob shook his head, smiling.

"Crazy kids. Did you find anything cool?"

The sun shone on their burnt faces. Wonder shone in their eyes.

"No," they said together at once.

19

They fell in love out there, on the third lake, beneath the surface, exploring the impossible house, diving together, improving the skills they learned in scuba class, eating lunches in the canoe, falling asleep in the canoe, sunning in the canoe, exploring each other's bodies in the canoe, too.

Eventually they stopped looking at the shoreline altogether. The shoreline was too close to reality, part of that real world they left behind every time they visited the third lake and the house that stood at its floor. They weren't quiet. They weren't hiding.

They played.

They played house.

Uncle Bob didn't ask again about the marks on the side of the canoe because James bought it from him before he could. Two dozen trips through the tight tunnel had stripped most of the green paint, leaving marks that might've been made by a giant water-cat, for all Bob knew. James saved up a hundred dollars working for his father, handed Uncle Bob the money, then handed him an additional ten bucks.

"What's this for?" Bob asked, the sun making him squint that day.

"For docking it here at your place."

"You don't have to do that, James."

"I know. But it's really nice of you to let us keep it here."

If Bob noticed any changes in the teenagers, he didn't mention it.

But James and Amelia weren't taking any chances. And if Bob or anybody else had asked what interested them *so much* about the lakes, about canoeing, both James and Amelia were prepared to lie.

"Lie," Amelia said one afternoon, the sun high above the mountains. They dangled their arms over the sides of the canoe, their fingertips grazed the crisp water.

"Absolutely," James said, his own eyes closed, his head resting on the front bench. They had books in the canoe, but neither read them. They were either down below or they weren't. And when they weren't they talked about being down below. "But it'd be easier if we didn't have to ... see everyone all the time."

"Like at work."

"Yeah. At home, too. You know what's easier than lying about what you're doing? Not seeing the people who are gonna ask you what you've been doing."

Amelia turned to face him. She had an idea.

"What about a raft?"

James opened his eyes. He looked to shore, noted the trees. They'd talked before about wanting a pontoon, something big enough to sprawl out on.

"We could anchor it to the roof," James said.

A bigger boat wouldn't fit through the tight tunnel. But building a platform, out here, and leaving it, could be just as good.

Could be better.

"We'll need an axe," James said. "And a lot of wood. Rope. The strong stuff."

"How big should we make it?"

"As big as we want to, I guess." James leaned forward and kissed her and the kiss lasted a long time. When he pulled away he was smiling. "You are *awesome*, Amelia. A raft."

Without discussion, they got back into their wetsuits, helped each other ready their tanks, secured their masks to their mouths, and dove into the third lake. Together they swam down to the half front door. They swam through the foyer, the dining room, the processions of lounges and the kitchen as big as Uncle Bob's cottage. They swam through the library, pausing at the bay window, shining their lights through the glass, pointing out fish that emerged from the murkiness, as bunnies might from a garden of flowers. They swam through every room on the lower floor and then, holding hands, they swam as fast as they could up the stairs, down the long hall with the single door. They swam into the dressing room and through the bedrooms and through an attic door in the second bedroom on the eastern side, swam up into the attic and through the tight eaves that wrapped around the attic like catacombs, like a single corridor, like the logical extension of the path they were on and had been since way back when Uncle Bob showed them the basics of the canoe he once owned. It all felt to them like the same moment, or perhaps, the same tunnel. Some parts were sunny, some were graffitied, but most of their journey was underwater, swimming deeper, deeper into the house.

20

They built the raft, a sturdy nine-by-six rectangle of uneven logs, held together with enough twine to form a second layer, a blanket of rope. They found their wood at the forested borders on shore. They dragged heavy timber through mud and overgrowth, carried them in tandem upon their shoulders, singing the song of the seven dwarfs. They cut one tree down. One. Because James believed the raft needed that one strong middle piece, so that if all else failed, if the rope somehow untied itself and all else drifted away, they'd still have that one solid trunk to hang on to, to rebuild around, to call home. They spent hours working, treading above the house, their bare feet close to the roof, almost close enough to stand on it. They took turns, exhausting themselves, laughing about it, debating it, happy to be making it, a place they could sleep, close to the house, so close that it was almost like owning it or maybe *just* like owning the house outright after all.

When they were finished, when the last knot was tied, Amelia secured one end of independent rope to the jutting end of the center log and James went under, swimming the rope around the home's short chimney, tucking it under the brick ridge at its zenith. It felt great, he told Amelia when he broke the surface again, sending ripples toward the canoe (toward the raft, too), felt like they had done yardwork, or built an extension, or, at the very least, had *added.*

"An addition to the house," Amelia said, laying a mattress pad and a blanket on the uneven logs.

James secured the canoe to the rope that held the raft to the house.

Then they sat on the edge of their raft and let their bare feet and ankles dangle in the water.

Amelia kissed him. She grabbed his face with both hands and kissed him until he leaned back, until he was lying down. She crawled upon him and kept kissing him and then James kissed her in return, running his hands over her shoulders, her lower back, her legs. The sun baked them from above as she straddled him. She took his hands and placed them on her breasts. James was breathing hard, tracing their shape beneath her bathing suit, squeezing them, kissing her neck. Amelia reached behind her back and untied the top, letting it slip past her shoulders, letting it fall to the logs that supported them. James kissed her breasts, tasted the lake water, wondered if every moment with Amelia would forever come coupled with the taste of the third lake.

They slid closer to the edge of the raft, James's hands upon her ass now, trying to roll her over, wanting so badly to get on top of her, to spread her legs apart, to feel the strength of her thighs against his body. He kissed her neck and shoulders and arms and eyelids and everything that showed. Amelia moaned in response and James finally did get her to lay down, on her back, and he bent at the waist to kiss her side, her thigh, to bite her. With his head toward the house, he looked over the edge of the raft, through the surface of the water, where the sun struck the roof, and he saw a single eye, looking back up at him, somebody crouched upon the roof of the house.

"*Oh fuck!*" James said, shoving himself toward the middle of the raft, away from the edge, away from Amelia, away from the water.

"What is it? What's wrong?" Amelia was up quick and on her knees now, crawling to the raft's edge. She saw the eye flitter, then vanish.

She stared. James crawled beside her and stared with her. Their shoulders touched but rather than feeling safe for being so close, they both leaned away from the contact.

Darkness below. Nothing on the roof.

Then a plop three feet from the raft and both screamed as a fish leapt out and sank quickly back into the water.

"Jesus!" James yelled.

There was a pause between them. As the water settled.

Then they both started laughing.

James had a hand on his naked chest and was alternately laughing and breathing hard, the way people do when they're not scared anymore, but some of the fright remains.

"Jesus," Amelia said. "You scared the shit out of me!"

"Well, I really thought I saw something for a second there."

"So did I. I saw a fish eye."

"So did I."

They laughed again. Amelia didn't make to cover her breasts and James couldn't stop looking at her. Didn't *want* to stop looking at her. They got on their bellies, side by side, their faces suspended over the edge of the raft. The sun was hot on their backs and their reflections were dark and rippling.

"Maybe it's a good thing that happened," Amelia said, speaking to James's warped reflection. James understood what she meant.

How close had they been?

Amelia breathed deep.

"You think we should do it in there?"

James stared at her dark reflection. Her eyes sparkled for a beat, then went black again.

"In the house?"

"Yes. Why not? It's special to us."

Special to us. This was true, but James could hardly believe they were talking about it at all, let alone the *where* of it.

"Our first time," he said. It would be the first time for either of them. "In the house."

"Yes."

He looked at her.

"That's possible, right?" he asked. "I mean … underwater … people can do that?"

"I think so."

Both seventeen. Both virgins. But both saying yes.

"Yes. Okay. Let's do it."

"Yes."

They didn't do it that day. Instead, they swam, they explored, they made adjustments to the raft, they ate lunch, they ate dinner, and they slept, for the first time, floating upon the third lake, in the darkness, listening to the crickets and frogs, a small symphony of life, crying out from the shoreline at the base of the mountains. They heard fish break the surface, plop back into the water. They thought of the oscillating eye they'd each seen down close to the roof. They watched the moonlight and were mesmerized by the patterns it made. There were hypnotic patterns in everything out there. The sounds, the smells, the sights. And the feelings, too, of holding one another, under a thin blanket, drifting.

But not from the house.

Drifting to sleep.

Tethered to the house.

Tied.

"I love you, Amelia," James whispered. But Amelia was already asleep. Already floating, in the middle of the third lake.

21

Amelia woke to the sound of splashing. But not quite splashing. More the sound of someone or something emerging, pulling itself out of the water.

Her left arm was asleep. She'd been laying on it. This always happened when she fell into a deep sleep. So, she rubbed her arm, shook it, tried to bring it back to life. James snored lightly on his back. She could see the tip of his nose in the moonlight. The rest of him was in shadow.

Amelia sat up. The water's surface was partially twinkling with scant moonlight. She could hear gentle waves lapping against the raft.

James rolled onto his side and fully vanished from sight. Like he'd wrapped himself up in the shadows, cold without them.

Amelia scanned the shoreline.

What woke her?

A fish, no doubt, just like the fish they'd seen leap near the raft after spotting its eye below the surface. Just a fish (*no doubt*). Except maybe a little doubt. A drop at least. Because it sounded like someone had either gotten out of the water or lowered themselves back in.

She watched for movement.

She listened.

She looked over James, beyond the edge of the raft, to where she knew the house to be. Tethered, they hadn't drifted, couldn't drift anymore.

But there was no sparkle of moonlight, no light at all over where the house must be and Amelia saw nothing.

She reached for her wetsuit and paused.

What was she thinking of doing? Diving at night? And if so ... would she tell James?

I just wanna know what made that sound. That's all.

But it was a strange motivation. What were the chances that the same fish that had woken her would be swimming through the halls of the house?

The vision of herself below, buried by all that moonless black, alternately thrilled and worried her. She wasn't sure *why* this should bother her at all. It wasn't any lighter inside the house during the day. Their flashlights provided one hundred percent of the light they used. So ... what was the difference between diving at noon or diving at night?

Possibly, Amelia thought, it was knowing that the world above was as dark as it was below, two layers of blindness, night upon night.

Endless black.

And yet ... the stars. Not as bright as she would've liked, but they certainly gave her something.

She looked to the edge of the raft, beyond her bare feet. She looked to shore. She looked to the surface of the lake, to the large area of impenetrable black that seemed to hover above the house (*our house*) like it was made of something more than water.

What was it about the stars that, no matter how they lit up the night sky, they couldn't remove the night?

Amelia stood up, carefully, aware that she could lose her balance, could misjudge the boundaries of the raft, could slip into the water.

This vision of her white body breaking the surface, herself as the one shimmering object in all this darkness, a beacon for whatever called the lake home, the lamp that the moths must get to.

She didn't like it.

Why not? Stop it. You're not scared. You love it here.

A stronger wave arrived and the canoe rocked audibly, tethered three feet away. She knelt at the edge of the raft and reached for the rope that held it. Then she drew it in, hand over hand.

As the canoe came closer, as its silhouette looked something like a dorsal fin, she realized fully that she was planning to check if their things were still in it. Clothes. The cooler. Books. As if they'd left their car unlocked outside a shopping mall, and not here in the middle of an otherwise uninhabited lake.

The canoe came the rest of the way too quick and banged hard against the raft. The sound of it made her jump.

You're not scared.

Amelia pulled the canoe broadside and reached in and felt for the cooler, their towels, their bags, their tanks, masks, and flippers.

She found the flashlights.

That's what you were looking for the whole time, wasn't it? Light.

She lifted one out of the canoe and turned it on.

She did not scan the canoe, James, or that starless patch of black that seemed to float above the house. Rather, she immediately trained the beam on the end of the raft, to where she believed she'd heard the sound that woke her.

"Fuck."

Beads of water shined at the foot of the logs, beyond James's feet and close to where her toes must have been when she was still asleep. She crawled to them, her hair hanging inches above the raft's edge.

In the light, they looked like tiny puddles. Proof that something had recently stood there.

Stood there?

Amelia didn't like the thought so she stopped thinking it.

You're not scared. You're sleeping on a raft in the middle of a lake. Things are going to get wet.

And yet ...

She bent her arm in a way so that she could come at the droplets from the lake's side of the edge. She dipped her fingertips into the tiny puddles. Then she laid her hand flat upon them. In a way, it fit. As if Amelia had made the watermarks herself. Or like someone had been holding onto the side of the raft, their legs dangling in the dark below.

Amelia inched away from the edge of the raft.

Stop it. You are not scared.

She'd heard of people, adults usually, intentionally turning a good thing into a bad thing. When things were going good, adults liked to ruin them. Her own mom called it a 'self-fulfilling prophecy.' And you did it to prove to yourself that it wasn't so good to begin with.

All this, the lake, James, the house ... this was a good thing.

So why was Amelia trying to ruin it?

She inched back to the mattress pad, sat, held her knees to her chest, scanned the shoreline. She turned the flashlight off, like she didn't want to draw attention to herself, didn't want to be the only thing lit up in all this darkness.

Night upon night. Darkness within. Darkness without.

The raft rose on a small wave and settled, tethered to a buried house.

"James?" she whispered, reaching into the shadows and tapping his shoulder.

James stirred.

"What's up?" he asked.

"James, what are these?"

"What are what?"

She shined the light on the edge of the raft. For a crazed beat she imagined someone might be there, a pair of wet eyes where the wood ended and the lake began.

James sat up.

"Those?"

"Yeah."

"It's water," he said.

"But how'd it get there?"

James thought about it. He wasn't scared. Amelia needed that.

"The canoe must've drifted. Hit the raft. Splashed it a little."

Amelia nodded.

"A lot of water out here," James said.

"Yes."

James got on his back again and fell immediately asleep. But Amelia stayed up, listening to the sound of the unseen waves lapping against the raft. Trying not to imagine them as fingers, or heads even, something with hands that hovered by the wood, waiting for her to sleep again, waiting for the darkness within her to match the darkness without.

22

Following Amelia through the house, the flippers propelling, James thought: *she's the coolest girl you've ever met.*

More than the bravery it took to explore the house was the fact that they were now spending nights on the raft.

Behind his mask, James smiled. He shined his beam in a circle around her until it looked like she was swimming through a ring of fire. She was performing for him; weaving through the halls, the rooms, up the stairs and down, through the attic, the bedrooms, and even sometimes above the seaweed gardens outside.

He owed a lot to this house. It'd given him something incredible to show her.

Still following her, he thought of her half naked body and the dozens of times he'd seen it. How soft her breasts felt in his hands, how sweet she tasted, the weight of her pressed upon him on the raft.

Could today be the day they lost their virginity in the house? And was it up to him to bring it up?

Maybe ...

Ahead, Amelia took a sudden left, entering the thin hall that connected the study to the kitchen, the vast magnificent kitchen with not one but two marble islands, where knives remained in their holders, the stove looked ready to use, and the cupboards were stocked with dishes, glasses, serving plates, and bowls.

All of it stationary. As if found in the kitchen of any dry home.

Glue? James asked himself. *Rope?*

But no *hows.* No *whys.*

Because of their one rule, their clubhouse guideline, James hadn't examined the dishes close enough to know *what* held them in place. In his father's hardware store they stocked sixteen types of glue. There was Glasgow wood glue strong enough to hold a cabin together. But you couldn't even hang a child's drawing on your wall with Duncle's. And the store had everything in between. In fact, James's dad would have so much to explain down here his head might explode from the excitement.

But would the pieces of his head fall to the floor ... or scatter freely about the house?

No hows. No whys.

Amelia said the house was kind of like the Garden of Eden. Neither of them gave a hoot about religion, but the analogy was spot on.

Don't eat the apple. Not down here.

But at seventeen years old, James *was* curious. He was far from the age when childhood's magic might return, far from being an old man who didn't *want* to ask questions, who happily accepted the unknown and all mysteries.

Probably it was because he spent most days talking to people about how things are put together, the best way to build, the best wood, tools, rubber and glue.

His father's hardware store constantly asked how and why.

It's how it survived. It's why it existed.

Home improvement.

Home.

And how one stays together.

Ahead, Amelia exited the kitchen by way of a spiral staircase that led to one of the bedrooms upstairs.

James didn't follow her.

Bringing his arms and legs up, he pushed himself to a stop. Bubbles rose from his facemask. He treaded above the two kitchen islands for a full minute. He thought about Eden. Then he lowered himself to the tiled kitchen floor.

On the counter was a small porcelain beaver. The three small holes on its back told James it was a pepper shaker.

Why isn't it floating? What's holding it down?

Training his light on the animal's teeth, James could sense the darkness behind him. It felt as if the entire house of darkness fanned out from this one point, this pepper shaker that somehow stayed put on the kitchen counter.

Some*how.*

The beaver's wide eyes seemed to stare up into the light.

James ran a finger along its back, over the holes.

He gripped it between his forefinger and thumb.

How.

He tugged.

For a beat it felt like it was going to come up with his hand. James could see the teeth, the eyes, the flat tail rising from the counter like any rational object should.

But it didn't move at all.

James's vision wasn't the best through the mask but it was good enough. Floating above the kitchen floor, he bent at the waist and examined where the shaker met the counter.

Being in the business of adhesives and tools, James had seen a hundred broken objects. He'd be able to spot a fix from across the kitchen. But there was no sign of glue at the base of the beaver.

James looked to the exit, to where he'd last seen Amelia swimming. For a breath he thought he saw her, arms crossed, eyes alight, no mask, no tank, no suit, watching him from across the kitchen.

He felt some shame for doing what he was doing.

He pulled on the shaker again. Harder this time.

No give.

No wiggle.

The shaker did not move.

James pulled a pocketknife from the small pouch secured around his waist. He popped it open. Holding the light with one hand, he wedged the knife where the shaker met the counter. He dug at it.

His flippers rose up behind him as he worked, until he was floating horizontal to the counter, his mask only a few inches from the beaver's teeth.

He dug at it again.

No wiggle.

No give.

James put the knife back in the pouch and swiveled toward the bigger knives. Their handles jutted out of their wooden holder.

He thought of Amelia. What she would say.

Why'd you need to know? This place is ours, James. Isn't that enough?

He looked back to the shaker, thinking maybe he should leave it alone.

But the shaker wasn't on the counter anymore.

"What?!"

The porcelain animal floated, eye level, and James watched it rotate in place, as if someone were turning it, showing him the bottom, showing him there was no evidence of glue.

James reached for it.

The shaker floated up, toward the ceiling.

James reached for it again and again it spun away.

He shined the beam in the space surrounding the shaker.

A pocket of cold water rolled the length of his body. James knew the feeling well. He'd experienced it in flooded basements, helping his dad repair a neighbor's pipes. Water so cold it seemed to grip you with actual fingers.

James sensed life behind him and turned quick.

A distorted face was inches from his own.

He yelled into his mask.

But it was Amelia.

Only Amelia.

Only.

She placed a hand on his shoulder. She was smiling.

She motioned for him to follow her. She was mouthing words. *A door,* she seemed to be saying. *A new door.* James held up a finger, telling her to hang on, he had something to show her, too.

But when he shined the light back to where the shaker had been, it was back, secure, on the counter.

The big teeth and dumb eyes glinted in his trembling beam.

Come on, Amelia seemed to be saying. *You're gonna love this.*

She swam from the kitchen and James followed.

23

While James was in the kitchen, studying the pepper shaker, Amelia had been doing flips, floating somersaults, through every room in the house. By the time she reached the lounge with the oil painting still life, she was dizzy from it, even a little turned around. She flipped once more and her flippers struck the wall and the wall opened and Amelia gasped, within her mask, understanding that, despite having explored the house a dozen times now, there were still new rooms to be found.

She swam into the surprise entrance and excitedly ran her beam in all directions, finding at first only a wall of chipped pink paint, possibly a closet. She shined the light to the floor, expecting (and hoping) to find shoes, evidence of someone having once lived here, like the floating dresses in the room upstairs.

But there were no shoes.

There were stairs.

Amelia treaded for half a minute, the word *basement* replaying in her mind. The word *impossible*, too, as the house (*our house*) was situated firmly in the muddy muck of the very bottom of the lake.

Finally, she swam toward the stairs, head down, her flippers clipping a light bulb's string above. But before fully diving into the subterranean level of the house, she stopped.

James.

She found him in the kitchen looking as if he'd seen a flesh and blood chef crawl into the oven and close the door. She convinced him to follow her.

Minutes later, treading above the staircase that, an hour before, neither of them had known existed, James thought the same two words Amelia had.

Basement.

Impossible.

But a third word worried him most.

Trapped.

As if, by swimming below, they wouldn't only have the lake above them.

They'd have the house, too.

Amelia swam first, head down. He watched her flippers vanish beyond the reach of his beam, into the throat of the stairwell.

Then he followed.

24

There were thirty steps in all. The stairwell was a tunnel of its own, traveling down at a dizzying angle. And like the concrete tunnel that delivered them to the third lake, there was graffiti.

Of a sort.

Rather than crude drawings of penises and naked women, the writing read like a growth chart, though neither James nor Amelia could fully envision a parent asking their child to stand against the wall, halfway down the basement stairs, in order to mark their height.

But there were marks. Rising marks. As if somebody's development had been noted.

After examining the marks for a minute, James and Amelia continued down.

Deeper.

At last, they arrived at an entrance to a wide room and Amelia felt another light bulb string trace her spine as she passed under it. She had to swim lower to avoid wooden support beams, the foundation of the home. She spotted a web, a large one, where one of the beams met the ceiling, and paused to show James. They treaded near it, studying the intricate design rippling with waves that must have come down the stairs with them.

A spider's web. Underwater. In a house at the bottom of a lake.

They continued, deeper, into the basement.

Space, James thought. The room had a lot of space. Amelia tugged on his wetsuit and pointed down with her beam, showing him a familiar flooring below. Blue and white tiles labeled with measurements, 3 ft., 5 ft., that in another context surely would have been clear but down here simply could not be.

And yet, as that which could not be *was* in this house, the basement proved no different.

Amelia and James treaded water six feet above an indoor pool.

With water all its own.

The surface moved independently of the water they swam in.

Amelia laughed and James could hear it, muffled by her mask, coming to him in marveled beats that perfectly embodied the wonder she was relishing.

Then she dove, swimming head first, into the pool.

25

It's warmer, Amelia thought. Warmer like an indoor pool ought to be. Like when somebody says it's *bath water. Bath water,* Amelia thought, soothing and smooth, enveloping, tomb-like, like a womb.

She rolled onto her back and sank to the concrete bottom. The tank struck first and she looked up through her mask, through the independent surface of the pool, into the lake water that held James, suspended so high above her.

Amelia smiled.

He looked so funny up there, treading, looking down at her, the bubbles rising beside him. Just then he looked like a man to her. The teenaged boy masked within.

James, she thought. *Come make love to me.*

They'd talked about it. She knew he was thinking about it, too.

Come make love to me.

She felt love for him then, the physical sensation of it leaving her body, rising up through the pool water, then through the lake water, traveling the light of his beam.

Suddenly James flipped, as though he'd felt the feelings she'd sent him. When his head was where his flippers had been, he swam toward her. Toward the swimming pool that should not be, had no *right* to be, but *was* all the same. Amelia embraced it. The magic. Frightening or not, it *was* magic. Water upon water, moving in different directions, the temperature in the pool warmer than the temperature out.

No *hows.* No *whys.*

Come to me ...

James broke the surface of the pool far to Amelia's right and through the fresh ripples he'd created, Amelia saw a form remained treading by the ceiling where he had been.

Amelia sat up fast. She planted her flippers solidly on the floor of the pool and rose. She stood half in the pool, half in the lake.

She pointed, up, to where James just was, breathing quicker now, shaking her head no, no there's nobody there, nobody treading where James just was.

James came to her as she had silently asked and wrapped his arms around her.

Amelia resisted, shoving him away, pointing to the ceiling with the beam of her light.

Look! She tried to say. *LOOK!*

But her voice was muted by the mask.

As if comprehending in slow motion, moving slower than the feeling of dread rising within him, James looked to where Amelia was frantically training her beam.

A black dress floated high above the indoor pool. Its dark fabric flapped with unseen waves. But its position is what scared James most.

Like someone's wearing it.

The hem rippled beneath the symmetrical shoulder straps, the waist was slimmer than the hips.

Amelia and James did not move. They did not cry out. They stared.

Then the dress started to sink, to fall toward them in the pool.

James wanted to believe it was chance, the way the dress seemed to be filled out, the way it looked.

Like someone's in it.

Like someone could swim up to it, then slip easily through the bottom, arms extended, with a mind to wear it.

Amelia held a hand in front of her mask.

James couldn't move. He was rooted to the floor of the pool's shallow end. As Amelia raised her other hand, blocked her face from the fabric, James watched the dress fold over upon itself, then twist in a way that no person could.

Not if someone was in it.

The dress floated away before it reached them.

Amelia lowered her arms and looked at James. They lit each other's masks with their respective beams.

"UP," James said.

Amelia nodded. And then James saw something more startling than the dress itself had been. In Amelia's face, James saw *fear.*

You're not supposed to be afraid, he thought. *You're the one that makes this all okay.*

But Amelia *was* scared.

And still ... she smiled. And the expression she wore was like that of a woman after a close call in a car.

Up, she mouthed. And they swam up. And as they exited the basement, James looked back, shined his light into the shadows, and saw no dress.

But he thought of it. Continuously, as they swam up the stairs, he thought of the black dress falling and how it hadn't looked like an errant article of clothing at the mercy of unseen undulations. No, it had behaved much more like a discarded dress that someone had taken off and tossed from the ceiling toward them.

26

They ate lunch on the raft. Turkey sandwiches and chips. Bottled water. They were exhausted. Diving itself was more of a workout than either of them usually got, but the experience in the basement took something extra out of them.

The sun felt good. Being above the surface felt good, too.

It always felt like night down in the house.

"You look good when you're tired," James said, his toes at the edge of the raft. Neither dangled their feet in the water.

"I was really scared for a second there."

"I know you were. I was, too."

The raft bobbed on steady undulations.

"I honestly thought somebody had found us," Amelia said. "I thought somebody had seen the canoe and came searching for us."

James wondered at this. He hadn't thought of it from that angle. Not at all. When he saw the dress floating above the pool his mind had gone to a much darker place than hers. And yet, maybe being found out was as dark a thing as Amelia could imagine.

"I love you," James suddenly said.

"I know you do. You didn't swim away when I was scared."

"Is that how somebody knows?"

James recalled how he felt immobile beneath the dress. How nothing in the world could have moved his flippers from the indoor pool.

Amelia smiled. It was good to see her smiling.

"That's how *I* know," she said.

They stared into each other's eyes, then Amelia looked down to the roof. James watched her breasts against the red fabric of her bikini top. Despite being so afraid less than half an hour ago, any movement of her muscle beneath her skin, any view of her skin at all, excited him.

Amelia suddenly kicked her feet to the edge of the raft and shoved off into the water. She swam out a few feet so that she was directly above the roof. She stared into James's eyes as she treaded water, the whole huge house beneath her.

It was a challenge, James thought. Something like one. Amelia was telling him she wasn't scared. Or perhaps she was telling herself.

We got spooked today, James thought. *So do we continue?*

This, he thought, was Amelia's way of saying yes. We continue.

He jumped in after her. For the first time since discovering the house he experienced that nerve burning sensation of something much bigger than himself beneath the water. Like the famous poster from *Jaws*, he was the very small swimmer cresting the surface, the many teeth of the house below.

When he reached her, they embraced. James did so partially out of fear. But Amelia, he could tell, had already moved on from the floating dress. They kissed and their mostly naked bodies pressed against one another, as their bare feet propelled them, kept them stationary above the roof of the house. Amelia stuck a hand deeper into the water and felt James's hard penis through his yellow bathing suit. She wanted to make love to him then, right there, high above their secret.

"Tomorrow," she whispered in his ear.

James pulled his face from hers. It was easier to forget about the basement now.

"Are you sure?"

"Yes," she said. "One hundred percent, yes."

They laughed because it was both awkward and assured. They laughed because they were embarrassed and they were brave, too.

These feelings warred and mingled within them both, as the water beneath experienced rotations of its own; pockets of warm, pockets of cold; pleasing water across their legs, their bellies, replaced, suddenly, by the icy tips of unseen fingers and the tips of tongues, tickling their bare skin from the deep, wanting perhaps to take hold of them, wanting to pull them deeper, deeper into the lake, deeper into the house, deeper in love, deeper ...

Tomorrow.

27

No wetsuits this time.

Just the masks, the flippers, the tanks.

And their bodies. Pale despite all the time spent on the lake. Pale because they spent their days below.

Below.

Today.

James and Amelia got ready on the raft. They didn't talk about it. They didn't say *today's the day*. No questions, no jokes, no assurances. James watched Amelia finish up, feeling almost hungry, watching her body move. Amelia watched James, too. The same hands that adjusted his mask would be holding her soon.

Below.

Beyond the edge of the raft, beneath the blue rippling surface of the water, the place of the coronation waited.

The house.

(*Home.*)

"All right," Amelia said, giving James a thumbs-up, a gesture she would have been embarrassed of only weeks before, when they first paddled out upon the lakes. "Ready."

She bent at the knee and dragged a toe across the surface of the water. It was warmer than most days. Welcoming.

"You look beautiful," James said.

Amelia shrugged and nodded, a weird thank you, then crouched at the edge of the raft.

But James jumped in first. His body broke the surface cleanly, creating sparkling ripples that reached for the logs and vanished quietly beneath them.

Amelia followed.

In truth, the water was colder without the wetsuits. But the shock of it woke them up a second time, and they clasped hands above the roof.

Then they plunged together, heads down, toward the half front door. At the muddy bottom their flippers sank and James climbed the mossy, slick step first. He held the half door open for her.

Amelia swam inside.

In the foyer they embraced. They couldn't kiss but that didn't stop them from running their hands over each other's bodies, frantic, mad, thirsty. Amelia gripped James's hard penis and pulled him toward her, pressing him against her belly, her thighs, her hips. They tumbled down the hall, horizontal to the floor, into the dining room, groping, crazed, hungry. Above the dining room table, but beneath the chandelier, they let go of their flashlights and the beams traced random patterns on the walls, exposing the room piecemeal; the glass cabinets, the vases like bookends on either side of the buffet, and their bathing suits, too, as they drifted from their now naked bodies.

The flashlights sunk to the table and there they remained, one trained upon the hall through which they'd come, the other upon the ceiling, a spotlight it seemed, mere inches from where they moved.

Floating, Amelia guided James inside her.

It wasn't easy. There was an art to this that neither of them knew.

And yet ... artless as it had to be, their clumsiness was perhaps most thrilling of all.

Entered for the first time, Amelia gasped, into her mask, and felt James tighten up. She relaxed him, rubbing her fingers against his shoulders, his back, his chest.

They made love in the darkness.

James's eyes were closed as he climaxed and Amelia felt him pull out, at the last moment, as he came.

In the beam of light beside them, they both saw the white cloud rise from the head of his penis, then spread, taken by unseen billows toward the ceiling, toward the walls, beyond the reach of the beam.

Amelia looked to James, his face partially lit by the fallen flashlight. She expected to see him wide-eyed, happy, deep love behind his mask. But James was looking up to the ceiling.

Slowly, Amelia reached for his chin, to turn his face toward hers, to connect. But without looking at her, he swiped her hand away and placed a single finger to his mask, telling her to be silent.

With his other hand he pointed to the ceiling.

Amelia looked up.

Then she heard it, too.

A ceiling creak. The unmistakable sound of footsteps above.

Like everything else in the house, the sound was distorted, the creaking was expanded to twice its natural width, and the feet Amelia imagined on the floor upstairs were not ones she wanted to see.

Then, laughter. As perverted as the creaking, single bone cackles rattled through the house, as if each syllable could swim.

James shook his head no.

It was the breaking point, the only thing more impossible than the existence of the house, than the items that clung to the counters, the walls, the floors.

They'd agreed never to ask *how* or *why*.

But neither had thought to ask *who?*

James grabbed Amelia by the wrist. He pulled her out from above the dining room table, into the hall, then the foyer, as the creaking continued above them, perhaps approaching the stairs.

And the androgynous laughter continued, too. Thick globules of sexless cheer.

Out through the half front door, James no longer pulled Amelia as she passed him, swimming fast, without their lights, climbing toward the surface of the lake.

Near the surface, James thought he heard a different kind of creaking. The unmistakable rasp of a (*crypt*) front door opening for the first time in forever.

He didn't look to the windows they passed. He didn't look down.

They broke the surface far from the raft, far from the roof, and swam for the logs fast.

Hurry, James thought, sensing something rising from below.

Amelia reached the raft first and she quickly pulled herself up.

James was seconds behind her. As his feet exited the water, a bubble burst behind him, a deep, tarred sound, and James told himself it was only (*laughter followed you up!*) a fish.

He tore his mask from his face. Amelia's mask already lay on the logs beside her.

"There's somebody in there," James said, pointing a shaking finger at the roof. Then he was on his knees, pulling the canoe to the raft.

"There's somebody in there," Amelia repeated, standing, staring into the water, leaning away from it, away from the house.

She stood that way, rooted, for as long as it took James to untie the canoe. She wiped the water from her pale skin. As if the droplets were alive.

"Come on," James said.

They were both afraid.

For the first time.

Afraid of the house.

"What do we do?' Amelia asked, still staring into the deep, to the roof of the house.

"We go," James said. "We go now."

28

A week.

A week without the house.

A fine, sunny, summer week. A perfect week to spend on a lake. Any lake.

But no.

Not the third lake and not the house.

For a week.

And counting.

Over the course of those seven days, James simply couldn't stop thinking about the house. When he took a shower he thought of the swimming pool in the basement. When he mowed the lawn he thought of the seaweed swaying outside the bay windows. When he walked the halls of his own home he felt a deep desire to bound, astronaut-like, *float* toward his bedroom. He wanted to tap the doors and watch them swing slowly inward. He missed the dreaminess, the impossibility. Even the fear.

A week.

A week without Amelia, too.

What happened? They'd lost their (*minds?*) virginity. They'd made love inside the house. Shouldn't they be celebrating? Shouldn't they be laughing about it? Shouldn't they be *talking?*

Yes, he knew they should be. The event should have brought them closer. Hell, the very night after they'd made love they should've gone to a diner, held one another in a booth, ordered too much or too little, as James ran his fingers through her drying auburn hair. But every time he went to text or call her he heard the creaking from above, the sound of somebody else in the house.

He couldn't get that elongated laughter out of his head.

He knew that Amelia had to be feeling the same way. About everything. Why else wouldn't she have called? And what did she feel worse about; the footsteps … or the sex?

James sat in a plastic chair on his back porch at night. Mom and Dad were asleep. It was impossible not to recall Amelia in the first silly suit, walking like a clumsy astronaut in the yard. He felt a tugging at his heart and he knew it was love. Knew it because so many people had felt it before him. This, he knew, was heartbreak.

Why not just call each other? Why not just *text?*

Because this isn't just heartbreak. There's the house to think about, too.

Other feelings, outside forces, fears. These were the enemies of a good thing. These were the problems people faced.

Fears.

James was scared. All day he was scared. All day he heard the creaking above, the slow thuds of something coming down a set of stairs. The sound of a half door creaking open behind him.

If they'd had their flashlights on their way up to the raft, what might James have seen below him in the beam?

He shifted uneasily on the porch chair. He sat forward and ran his fingers through his hair. He felt like he fucked something up. Like he crushed a delicate object.

Everything was going *so* well. They'd made love in the house! How much more memorable could it get?

It's the house, man. She's not texting you cause she's trying to stay away from the house.

James kicked at an empty cooler beside him on the porch. Then he kicked at it again. Then he got up and kicked it once more, halfway across the yard. He followed it, and kicked it again.

WHAT HAPPENED?!

He knelt beside the cooler with a mind to rear the thing apart, then stopped.

Call her. She's angry, too.

He got up and crossed the yard. His phone was sitting on the barbecue. He grabbed it and called, without planning what he'd say, without thinking that by calling her he might be pointing them both toward the house.

And that laughter. Do you remember it? Remember how it followed you up out of the water? How it splashed?

Ringing. Ringing. Ringing.

His heart hammered and he felt light headed and he knew, quite suddenly, exactly what he was going to say.

"Hello?"

Amelia's voice. Amelia awake.

"Amelia. I love you. Everything's fine. We're both scared. But let's be scared together. Let's—"

"Got you! I'm not here. Leave a message, sucka!"

Fuck.

He set his phone back on the barbecue. Then kicked the barbecue hard.

An animal moved in the evergreens bordering his yard and James looked into the darkness, wished he had a flashlight, wished he was exploring an impossibly furnished darkness instead.

He picked up his phone and took it inside. It was dark, but not dark enough. Quiet, but not the good kind, not the kind of quiet that included waves, water washing over you.

A week.

James entered his bedroom. He didn't turn on the light. He didn't clear the scuba masks and flippers from his bed. He flopped onto the mattress, face down, and stared into the darkness of his pillow for a few minutes.

He wondered if this was the moment in which he was supposed to move on. Like the songs said. A man with a broken heart was supposed to move on. Sometimes things just got too complicated. Something unwanted was added to something wanted and blew the whole thing apart.

Fear.

Fear of the house. Fear of the stretched laughter. Fear of what they'd done together. Fear of who lived there.

Who?

He rolled onto his back, set the phone on the windowsill above his head, crossed his arms over his chest, and drifted.

Drifted like they once drifted on a canoe. Amelia and James. Anxious, laughing, exploring, falling in love.

Maybe Amelia already moved on. That was okay if she had. It meant she was smarter than him. Saw something scary and stepped aside. Isn't that what everybody was taught to do?

Hear a scary sound in a house ... leave the house.

Drifting.

Floating in a banged up canoe on a dangerous third lake. No signs along the shoreline out there, no warning for swimmers:

NO SWIMMING:

A HOUSE AT THE BOTTOM OF THE LAKE

A house you'll wanna explore. A house you'll wanna call home.

James dreamt of the pepper shaker. He was knifing its base and when Amelia appeared behind him to tell him about the basement door, she was crying.

What is it? James asked in cartoon bubbles.

You ruined it, she answered. *You ruined it by asking how. Why did you ask how? Why did you ask anything at all when everything was so good?*

I'm sorry, James said, reaching out for her in the dark water. *I didn't mean to do it!*

Amelia drifted, back into the shadows, crying, shaking her head no, *it's ruined it's ruined, we're scared now, don't you see we're scared?*

Amelia!

Amelia was gone. Swallowed by the kitchen shadows.

But someone remained. A formless figure, vague as melted wax.

Who are you? James asked.

A face without features emerged from the wallpaper. No eyes, only folds, more wrinkles than his bed sheets, skin grayer than what was under the green paint of the canoe.

It's just a fish, James said. *You're just a fish!*

Wide watery eyes. Fat boxer lips.

A woman? No. A man?

Please.

And a dress. What color? Couldn't tell. A fish in a dress? No fish. A woman?

No woman.

Amelia! James screamed, but the bloated body, stuffed into a dress too small, was stepping out of the shadows, lips flapping in the unseen waves in the kitchen.

AMELIA!!

Lipstick. Heels. Fat, wrinkled knees. Couldn't stand in the heels. Didn't know it wasn't walking right. Thought it was gorgeous. Thought it was—

AMELIA!!!

Chapped fingers took James's hands, tugging, flirtatious, toward the dining room, toward the first time, toward sex.

James pulled back but he couldn't extricate his fingers. Like the pepper shaker on the kitchen counter. Held there. Stuck there.

How?!

And that laughter again. Bass drum beats made of taffy.

James closed his eyes in his dream and screamed because he could still see it, could still see the (*man, woman, makes no difference down here*) fish-thing drawing him to it, and closed his eyes within his eyes and screamed again.

And woke.

Woke in his bedroom.

Wet.

Wet dream?

No.

He sat up and pressed his palms to the blanket beneath him.

Not wet.

Soaked.

When he pulled his hands from the blanket he saw his arms were wet. He turned his head quick and water fell from his brow. His hair was flattened to his brow. His bedroom, his things...

James wiped water from his eyes and saw.

Three inches of water on the carpeted floor. Books and figurines that should've been on the dresser, *were* on the dresser, were now on the floor.

A *shipwreck,* James thought.

A sunken bedroom.

Underwater overnight.

"*Mom! DAD!*"

Water everywhere. Dripping from the ceiling, dripping down the walls. On the windowsill, his phone sat in a puddle.

James leaped from his bed and splashed onto the floor. He lost his footing and fell, into the water, three inches deep. Warm water. He was used to it. As if he'd spent the night (*the summer*) in it.

He scrambled and grabbed his phone from the windowsill.

He called Amelia.

"Hello?"

Voicemail.

Where was she? *Where was she?!*

Crazed, he sloshed out of his bedroom. In the hall he peered back in. He felt something he knew shouldn't be happy to feel. It was relief. Relief that it was all still happening.

The impossibilities.

The magic.

He called Amelia again.

No response.

Water everywhere in his bedroom. But no water in the hall. No water anywhere else. Only his bedroom. Submerged overnight. While he was sleeping.

Sunk.

James was awake. Wide awake.

What happened here?

Fear.

A deeper fear. A new fear. No longer just afraid of the house. The house was over *there.* Underwater. But this ... his bedroom was miles from the lake ... this was his parents' home. This was bad. This was putting other people in danger. How could he keep *this* a secret?

This was *bad.*

James hurried out of the house. The sunny afternoon frightened him. Too bright. Too exposed. Too normal.

He tried to calm down. He breathed. The sun dried his shorts, his shirt, his hair. He called Dad on his cellphone.

Dad answered.

"You all right, James?"

"No. There was a ... did there ... did a pipe break or something?"

"What do you mean?"

"My room is soaking wet."

"Your bedroom?"

"Yeah. Soaking wet, Dad."

"Anywhere else in the house?"

"No. Just my room. What do you think it was?"

"I know what it was. A water main."

"How do you know that's what it was? How do you know that?"

Fear in his voice. New fear. Scared of everything.

"What else could it have been?" Dad said. Then he half chuckled. James thought of laughter rising like bubbles in a lake. "It didn't rain last night."

What else could it have been, James? What else?

"Okay. What do I do?"

"Nothing. I'll send Dana."

"Okay. What should I ... I shouldn't go back in there."

"What do you mean?"

"I mean ... in the house. I should probably wait for Dana?"

Dad laughed.

"It's not going to kill you, James. It's a water main. But wait wherever you want. I'll send Dana and she'll fix it."

"Thanks, Dad."

"You all right, James?"

"Yeah, just ..." fear in his voice fear in his blood, "... kinda freaky to wake up that way."

"I imagine so. Anything ruined?"

"No. I mean ... nothing important. Just ... I don't know."

"Well check it out. You don't wanna lose everything."

"Okay, Dad. Yes. Thank you."

They hung up.

James looked up to the blue sky. Down to the dry, green grass.

You don't wanna lose everything.

But he had. He'd lost everything.

The house.

Amelia.

Everything.

And yet ... was it still going on?

The house? Amelia? Everything?

By the time Dana pulled her work van into the drive, James was sitting cross-legged at the end of the driveway. Dana would later tell James's dad that it was like pulling up on someone sitting on a raft, tethered to a house. As if James wanted to get away, but was afraid of being lost at sea.

29

Stocking the shelves at Darlene's, Amelia knew better than to try and push the house out of her mind. There was no use fighting it. She was obsessed, and if there was one thing her mother had taught her about obsession it was, *even when you don't you do.*

In the week since they left the third lake, Amelia *did*. She *did* think about the cool water lapping against the wood of the raft. She *did* think about how good it felt to be *on* that raft, James's eyes traveling up and down her body like the flowery fountain in the front of the Chinese restaurant in town. Up and down. Over and over. His interest recycled with every revolution. She missed it. She missed the logs beneath her bare feet, the superhero feeling of slipping into the wetsuit for the first time each day, the shine of the mountains framing the third lake. She missed the sun, the sounds, the sensations.

But most of all, she missed the house.

Marcy spoke over the grocery store's loudspeaker:

"There's been a spill of boogers in aisle three. Amelia? Can you take care of that?"

Amelia tried to smile. It was hard. The store was empty and Marcy was trying to help. She knew Amelia was going through something, but she didn't know exactly what.

Even now, crestfallen, scared, confused, Amelia didn't talk about the house.

Or the noise upstairs.

A week.

A week without smoke could drive a smoker mad. A week without family could change a man.

Amelia felt changed. Different. Afraid.

"Amelia?"

Stocking rice in aisle three, Amelia turned to see Marcy, twirling the ends of her hair until she'd made two handlebars extending far from her head. She chomped her gum like a dog.

"Do I look like one big mustache?"

Amelia tried to smile. It was hard.

Seeing Marcy's hair unnaturally fanned out like that made her think of her own in the mirrors of the house.

"Are you *really* okay, Amelia?"

Amelia looked down to her hands and saw she was holding a box of cereal. In the rice aisle. *How'd that get here?*

"I'm fine."

"You've been in this aisle for close to ten minutes. And you're stocking wrong."

The cereal doesn't belong here, Amelia. And you don't belong in the house.

"Sorry," she said. "I'll get it together, Marcy."

"Is it because you're in love?"

At the mention of the word, Amelia could see James, mid-flight, diving into the water above the roof.

"Just a bit tired," she said.

"Nu uh," Marcy said, shaking her head no.

Amelia saw the bottom of James's bare feet as he was swallowed by the darkness of the lake.

"Come on, Marcy. I'm fine."

"Okay. But if you spend another ten minutes in here, I'm calling the heartbreak police."

Amelia tried to smile. It was hard.

Marcy left her.

Amelia crouched and set the cereal on the ground beside the box of rice. She thought of James's sperm, fanning out, a slow-mo explosion, how cool it looked, how amazing everything was up until then ... up until exactly then.

Amelia opened the box of rice and heard Marcy goofing off in the next aisle. It sounded like she was ... squishing something. Wringing out a rag. Something wet.

Has she ever lost everything? Amelia thought. *Everything all at once?*

It sounded like Marcy dropped something. A wet plopping sound. It had the unmistakable tone of a friend sneaking up on you.

"Careful, Marcy," she called.

A second plop. This one louder. Sounded to Amelia like wet shoes.

"Marcy?"

Sometimes, after you'd come back in from taking out the trash, your shoes squeaked on the grocery store's linoleum floor. It was joke amongst the coworkers. *Watch out for slime out by the dumpster. It likes you. It's gonna follow you back in.*

Another squish from the aisle over and Amelia felt the first real wave of fear. It did come like that, in a wave, not from her mind to her body, but rather like the unseen waves beneath the surface of the third lake; it attacked your face and front first, then wrapped itself around the rest of you.

"Marcy?"

Another slow wet step. As if the person wearing the wet shoes didn't know exactly how to walk.

Or like they haven't walked on dry land in a long, long time, Amelia.

"*Marcy?!*"

Tears started to blur the bottom of Amelia's eyes. She looked up, slowly, to the round security mirror hanging from the grocery store ceiling.

Was there something in the aisle over? Was there?

"Amelia! What's wrong with you today?"

Marcy. Behind her. At the end of the aisle.

Another wet step. Approaching the far end of the aisle over.

"What is that sound, Marcy?" Amelia asked, her eyes bright and afraid.

"What sound?"

Amelia got up. She looked to the opposite end of the aisle, where whoever walked on the other side would no doubt show, would no doubt come sloshing for Amelia.

"Oh Jesus, Marcy. I have to go."

"*Go?* Are you crazy, Amelia?"

Amelia backed up to Marcy, felt her behind her, but didn't take her eyes off the end of the aisle.

"I'm sorry," she said, her voice shaking. "I have to go. I have to go. Now."

"Amelia, you can't—"

Amelia gasped as a woman passed the end of the aisle. She was wearing a green tank top and bright orange shorts. Sunglasses and a visor. She carried a snorkel she'd just taken from the aisle over and her flip-flops made squishy sounds as she passed.

Amelia looked at Marcy.

Then she broke out laughing. It wasn't hard to do.

"Amelia, what the *hell?*"

Then, Amelia's name again, this time spoken from the end of the aisle where the woman just passed.

"Amelia."

A boy's voice.

Before turning to face him, Amelia knew who it was. How could she not? She'd replayed his voice a thousand times over the last week.

"James."

James stood shame-faced at end of the aisle.

No, Amelia thought. *Not shame. Fear.*

"I'm sorry I came to your work," he said. "But it came to my house last night."

Amelia didn't respond. Not directly.

"Marcy," she said, still staring at James. Her voice was firm, the firmest it'd been in a week. "Can you leave us alone for a minute?"

"Sure thing."

Then Marcy slipped out of the aisle behind her and Amelia and James faced one another in silence.

It came to my house last night.

And no response from Amelia. As if she wasn't surprised.

We left the lake, they both thought, in their own words. *But the lake wants us back.*

One week.

One week apart.

Amelia rushed to him.

She hugged him hard. All of her warring emotions found room to breathe and she cried. But she smiled, too. James gently held the back of her head and pulled her close, closer, until it felt like nothing could pull her from his grip again. Not even waves.

"James," she said. "James, are we going crazy?"

"We need a third party," he said. "We need to tell someone."

"No," Amelia said. "Not that."

James looked deep into her eyes. Were he and Amelia at the same place with this? Or was Amelia somewhere deeper?

"Then what? What do we do?"

"Hear me out," she said, pulling her head from his chest. Facing him.

"Okay. What?"

She paused. She breathed deep. And she told him.

"We need to go back."

"Amelia ..."

"We need to introduce ourselves, James. We need to say hello."

James held her. He'd come to Darlene's with a mind to do whatever it was Amelia thought they should do. But he couldn't hold onto the word *hello* and it slipped from between his fingers and splattered, wet, to the grocery store floor.

"Okay," he said, loving her, in love with her, wanting her to be happy. "Okay."

But as she hugged him he understood that he wasn't just doing what Amelia wanted to do. The moment he said *okay* he'd felt a relief he hadn't known in seven days.

No, Amelia wasn't in any deeper than James was. She'd just figured out a reason to do exactly what he wanted so badly to do.

To go back.

Back to the house.

We should introduce ourselves. We need to say hello.

"Do you think it will welcome us?" he asked, horror and relief somehow mingling in his blood.

Amelia nodded.

"We live there, too, James. *We live there, too.*"

30

Paddling across the first lake felt different because they were paddling toward some *thing*, not some place.

Squeezing through the graffitied tunnel felt different because they pushed in order to reach some *thing*, not some place.

And standing on the raft, looking down into the water, felt different because they both believed something was looking back, through the windows of that wonderful, magic place below.

31

James dove in first, no doubt in an effort to show Amelia he was on board with her idea, though he didn't feel much different inside. And yet, the moment his shoulders split the cool water, as the surface spread like lips, sucking him in, James understood there was really no other option. Because the only other thing to do would be to *not come back*. And they couldn't do that. They *wouldn't* do that. This was their clubhouse, their tree-house, their secret, *theirs*.

Swimming toward the muddy lake floor, sensing Amelia had broken the surface above him, James recalled a time when he was ten years old. He and some friends had a clubhouse of their own. They called it Potscrubber and Potscrubber was no more than a huge cardboard box, cut open, placed against two trees, creating a bivouac, shelter for their secrets, too. The box itself had once been used for a dishwashing machine and the label *Potscrubber* was on the inside of the clubhouse, always in sight.

James reached the bottom, lowered his flippers to the mud, and felt the familiar sinking, the becoming one with the foundation of the plot.

Their plot.

He thought of the spider they found in Potscrubber.

Derrick looked it up in his encyclopedia and said it was poisonous. Called it a brown recluse and said one bite could kill a man. Jerry said Derrick had the wrong spider, said they looked alike but that wasn't it. Derrick didn't want to go back. Said they should leave Potscrubber, too, just leave it there in the woods. Wasn't any good anymore.

But Jerry wanted to get rid of it. And so did James.

The friends returned to Potscrubber.

Amelia touched down beside him and they turned to face the house together. They shined their lights into the darkness on either side of the house first, as if looking for (*someone in the yard*) movement. Their beams extended into forever, or nothingness, as both felt the same. They illuminated the front windows. They were very aware that they were looking for someone. Checking (*is anybody home?*) for faces. That's what they were there to do.

To introduce ourselves.

James thought of the spider bites on Jerry's arms and legs. The chunks the doctors had to take out of Jerry's right thigh and left bicep. How his clothes hung slack ever after.

Amelia tapped James on the shoulder.

Are you ready? She seemed to be asking.

James nodded. He was ready.

Amelia swam ahead, through the half front door.

James followed.

In his light, flecks of mud rose in a circle around her flippers. In *her* light, he saw the inside of the house, piecemeal, in parts. It had been a week. A week without.

It felt savory, the brief images, *relief.*

Suddenly, Amelia turned around and swam back to James. She gripped him by the sides of his head and pressed her mask against his. Peace. James and Amelia. Back underwater. Back in the house.

What had he lost after all? Nothing. He'd lost nothing.

Amelia said something, words he couldn't understand. Then she was off. Swimming into the darkness.

And James followed.

Deeper.

Deepest yet.

32

Inside, swimming apart, then together, Amelia vanished behind a partially opened door, James paused to shine his light under the pool table, into the corners, the murky blackness falling in, *rolling* in, whenever he drew the light away. Amelia saw it, saw the darkness at bay, saw the darkness return, by the flickering, anxious movements of James's light. James saw it, too, saw the edges of the dark like physical planes, touchable down here, *always* down here. He saw it gripping the beam of Amelia's light like black hands, black lips, swallowing.

The darkness was present, even when it was lit.

Through the study, the lounges, the library, the kitchen, where James had gotten scared by the pepper shaker. Into the Florida room, walls of glass looking out into the murky depths, fish swimming past, through their wavering beams, fish no more colorful than the water, than the dull rippling grays and blacks, blending in, not wanting to be seen, not wanting to be met. Flecks of mud floating like dust above a dirt road, unseen footsteps bringing it up, bringing it to life. James and Amelia paused here, pressing their beams to the glass, feeling small in size, in comparison to the boundaryless body of the mountains, the lake, the house.

They once imagined gardens of their own growing in that lifeless mud; colorless flowers swaying in the under-waves.

Were these dreams still possible? Was everything possible now?

They swam on, swerving through the halls, avoiding lamps, dressers, swimming up to over couches, diving below chandeliers and light bulbs alike. At the basement door, Amelia paused and looked James in the eye. She shined the light on her own face and mouthed the word *sauna.* And though James hadn't thought about it himself since they saw it, he knew what door she was referring to. The closed wooden door by the indoor pool. The one room they hadn't checked in the house. Would they find the object of their search there? A towel around its waist, sweat pouring from its impossible brow?

Behind the basement door and well below it, a swimming pool sat in complete darkness, its water somehow untangled from the water of the lake. Maybe they'd find it there. Wading waiting, waiting wading.

"Sauna," James said and Amelia pushed open the basement door. James followed her into the darkness. He followed her down the stairs, hearing in his memory the things she'd recently said. He used her words to battle through the rising curtain of bad feelings, the idea that they shouldn't be here, that this wasn't just love anymore.

This was danger.

But the elixir of being inside the house again made it easier to shove these fears aside.

Down the stone steps they swam, beneath the low hanging support beams, until their flashlights revealed the rippling waters below. It flowed in the opposite direction of the water they swam in, as if the ghost of a second moon orbited the pool, causing a second tide.

Just past the pool, Amelia shined her light upon the smooth wood door of the sauna.

James thought of Potscrubber. He couldn't help it.

Amelia placed a hand on the sauna door.

James gripped her wrist. When she turned to face him he saw the obsession in her eyes.

Jerry, he remembered saying, as the walls of Potscrubber trembled on their own, *there's another one on your shoulder.*

"Be careful," James said. But it came out unintelligible. A useless warning. One he wasn't adhering to himself.

And yet, Amelia must have read his lips for she responded in kind.

"Of course."

Then she smiled and gave him that same thumbs-up. This time without shame.

Here we go, she seemed to say. *Where we've been going all along.*

She pushed gently on the wood and the door opened.

They entered the sauna and their lights revealed empty wooden benches. A cold stove.

But James felt hot.

He shined the light upon the stove, convinced it had to be on after all, sure that the sauna was functioning, inexplicably, like everything else in the house. He looked over his shoulder in time to see the door slowly swinging closed, like every other door, riding the unseen undulations at the bottom of the lake. But this time it felt different. It looked different, too.

Deliberate? James thought. But it was not a question, rather an elusive word finally found. *Someone is closing the door. We're going to boil to death in here.*

His mask began to fog.

Fear?

Heat?

He grabbed Amelia by the arm and swam toward the closing door, dragging her until she swam on her own, James leading the way now, his palm against the wood, pressing back, pushing hard, expecting resistance, and finding none.

The door swung open, easily. James shined his light behind it.

Nobody.

Nothing.

Not here.

But somebody.

Upstairs.

James and Amelia looked up together, to the familiar sound of the ceiling creaking.

A thudding above. Sluggish.

Deliberate.

Had it tried to trap them? And would it try to again?

They followed the sound with their eyes, treading above the pool, then the tiles bordering the pool, as the wide creaking steps drifted farther from them, heading, it seemed, to the basement door.

Without hesitation, Amelia swam toward it. Toward the approaching sound.

At first, James couldn't move. Didn't *want* to move. Whatever was in this house was approaching, was near, and though they had agreed to greet it, James found that when the moment was upon him, the agreement seemed insane. Frozen with indecision, he watched her grow smaller. His fear expanded. And even then, as Amelia went *to* the sound, to the beat of his horror, he didn't want to be alone, didn't want to float here, tread by the sauna alone. James went to her, to catch her, to catch up, aware of the open space behind him, the growing space.

Ahead, Amelia vanished, up the stairs.

We should introduce ourselves.

And so she was.

James entered the stone corridor of stairs, felt the pressure of the growing space behind him. His arms and legs tingled, like when a child races up from the basement, sure that something wet, something *old*, was seconds away from taking hold of his ankle.

Come back, James, it would say, the words as bloated as its face. *Stay a little longer.*

Oh, the feeling that something was near, was closing in, would grab him and drag him flailing back to the sauna where this time the door would close, the door would lock, where James would boil to death, screaming inside his mask, boiling, burning, blistering.

The growing space.

He swam up the stairs and it felt like running uphill, the resistance, the fatigue, the impatience of a nightmare. Amelia was out of range, out of sight. He called to her, but his words were a series of useless bubbles that popped against the interior of the mask in rhythm with the elongated thuds from the ceiling.

The ceiling.

The ceiling.

Where the creaks continued. Where the sound of wide steps went on.

James reached the top of the stairs and crashed through the door. The thudding went on, the steps, pounding in his head, pounding in his bones; the beat of dead skins stretched taut across steel drums made from the body of a battered canoe.

He reached out, into the darkness, hoping to find her, to pull Amelia away from whatever made that sound, whatever was coming, whatever she wanted so desperately to meet.

We went crazy, James thought. *We went crazy in love.*

The thought was clear, defined, despite the frantic ramble around him. He shined his light manic throughout the room. To the two doors, two exits, both partially open. To the chairs and the cushions that did not float above them. To the end table and the ashtray that did not float above it. To the shelves where books in impossible condition did not succumb to the laws of nature. To the ceiling where solid wood beams did not wither to chips.

No Amelia.

Not here.

But the beat, *still* drumming, went on.

James swam toward one of the doors.

Stopped. (The water rushed past him.)

Turned. (The water turned with him.)

Swam toward the other.

Stopped. (The water rushed past him.)

Turned. (The water turned with him.)

Where was it coming from? Where was Amelia? How close was she to meeting the monster?

Had she met it already?

Movement behind and James turned once more, quick, shining his light on the portrait, the still-life hanging on the wall. He recoiled from the face it made, the table-edge mouth and the curtains for hair. The plums for eyes and the life in their stare.

The canvas rippled, sending an expression across the painting.

The purple eyes seemed to focus. The mouth bulged out toward him.

James dropped his flashlight.

He flipped toward the floor, reaching for the light as it sank.

Sank.

Sank.

Connected with the floor.

Went black.

Black.

Black.

Something touched him.

Wet canvas? The pulp of rotten fruit?

James reached the carpeted floor and curled up, hands high, protecting him from anything in the room.

(*The bulging painting, coming to life, leaving the wall behind.*)

Amelia!

Amelia who was somewhere else in the house, intentionally approaching the danger.

Amelia!

Amelia who went to meet whatever was responsible for the drum-thudding, thud-drumming of his heart.

"Amelia! Help!"

He was floating now, floating toward the bay window, fast enough, it seemed, to break it, powerful enough to crash through the glass, to be sent spiraling out into the lake, zero gravity, spinning, farther from the house, farther from (*everything*) Amelia.

"Amelia!!"

He'd seen the table-edge mouth parting. Before the world went black. He'd seen the plum eyes registering his presence in the room. Before the world went black.

I'm not gonna make it, James thought. *I'm not gonna make it OUT OF THIS HOUSE.*

Paralyzed with fright, curled into a ball and free-floating near the ceiling of the lounge, James understood it was the most scared he'd ever been in his entire life. And while he always dreamed he'd perform with honor if ever he was this afraid, he'd underestimated how afraid *this* was.

And yet, what came next was the only thing that could have frightened him more than he already was.

It was the scariest thing that could happen inside a house underwater, a house at the bottom of a lake.

The lights came on.

Not the flashlight.

The house lights.

The lights in the ceiling. The lights in the halls. The lights on every window and wall.

The lights came on.

And James *saw.*

James saw the room, bathed, exposed. Saw the vibrant, breathing color of the house.

In the bay window he saw himself reflected. Curled up, floating, scared.

Exposed.

The lights are on.

The lamp on the end table was on.

On.

A burning bulb.

Electricity.

Running.

Underwater.

On.

33

Amelia placed both hands on the basement door and pushed hard, too excited to stop, following the thudding steps she'd heard overhead. James was still below, she knew, but he must be coming. She didn't mean to leave him behind, but the steps led her here, into the lounge. This was *exactly* where they were leading, two points converging, herself and the steps, to meet (at last) here in the lounge.

But when she got there, her light showed her that she was alone.

"Hello?"

The two syllables collapsed flat in the mask.

Then she heard the creaking again from outside the lounge and Amelia understood that she'd just arrived a little late was all.

Whoever she was supposed to meet was simply ahead of her.

Deeper into the house.

Amelia swam, hurriedly, toward the door to her left. She thought James must be close. He'd know to follow her. He'd find the lounge empty and follow her and either way, no matter what *he* did *she* had to get moving, had to catch up with whoever was still moving ahead.

She passed through the door as it swayed shut. But whoever had been in this adjacent room was now in the next.

The steps told her so.

Amelia followed.

Her flashlight flickered and she knew that it was dying. Knew that it would go out, go black if she didn't get up to the raft and change the batteries. And yet, there was a part of her that believed it would go black even if the batteries were new.

You're in bigger hands than your own, she thought, without knowing (or caring) exactly what this meant to her.

The thudding continued. Growing dimmer.

She followed her dying beam from room to room, avoiding the objects of each, until it felt like a dance, an intentional movement, between herself and the other. Because the light was dimming, she could no longer see the corners, not seven feet in front of her mask. And the house, it seemed, was growing darker, dimming, a purposeful setting of a mood.

Into the kitchen, over the first marble island, then close to the kitchen floor, then up past a window in quadrants. All of this in flickering pieces, graying sights, near darkness.

Soon she couldn't tell what room she was in, what thresholds she crossed.

And yet, she continued, pursuing the source of those steps, until, at last, she saw the foot of the stairs ahead.

The light dimmed.

She treaded above the bottom step, listening for the other.

Where had it gone?

Up?

A creaking on the stairs told her how close she was, but her light showed her no form.

She should wait for James, she thought. Wait for more light. Wait.

But she couldn't.

She swam up the stairs, above them, rising to the second floor, following the creaking of the wood, the creaking of the old house, the thud-drumming, drum-thudding of bare wet feet sloshing up the steps.

Halfway up the stairs her flashlight died.

Darkness.

Complete darkness in the house.

For the first time, Amelia experienced the house as it was without her and James, as it stood at night, how it was before they arrived.

She was guided by the creaking, and she understood she was at the top of the stairs, entering the hall, the long hall with a single swaying door at its far end, a door she could hear opening ahead.

She swam, into the darkness, deeper into the throat of the second story, her hands straight out, ready to connect.

Amelia thought she could hear fabric in the darkness, tugged on, sliding off the smooth curved shoulder of a wooden hanger.

She released her flashlight. Useless now.

And though she couldn't see it, she could *sense* it sinking, sinking, until it hardly nicked the second story floor, contact as slight as a brush.

And then the lights came on.

Not the meager beam of her flashlight, no.

The house lights came on.

Amelia stopped swimming (the water rushed past her), not meaning to, but overwhelmed by it, astonished, seeing for the first time the hall walls in detail, the exact colors, lines, and dimensions of the house.

Floating, breathless, she looked over her shoulder to the top of the stairs. She saw the runner was red, bright red, the color of exaggerated blood. Light came from downstairs and she understood, clearly, that the second story hall wasn't the only place lit up.

The house. The entire house.

She positioned herself so that she was facing the door at the end of the hall again.

Staring ahead, treading, Amelia smiled as much as her mask would allow.

She knew why the lights came on. She hadn't asked why, she hadn't let herself do that, but she *understood*.

It was an offering. A welcoming.

A greeting.

She swam.

She reached the door. She saw the details of the door, smudge marks (*wax?*) where other fingers (*not your own!*) had opened the door before her.

Amelia entered the dressing room. She saw the color red as it came floating toward her. She ducked, allowing the red fabric to pass over her, the red dress, a curtain parting to reveal the stage, the space before the opened wardrobe doors.

A woman.

No.

A form.

Naked.

How old?

Couldn't see its face, its back was to Amelia.

No.

Could see its face. Reflected in a mirror hanging inside the wardrobe door.

No face.

Amelia floated toward the thing, propelled by unseen waves.

Wax.

The word felt silly, a foolish way to describe what stood before her and yet, it *did* look made of wax.

Like when you melt wax and then dip it in water.

No face. No hair. No bones. Only undefined mounds of pink, thick molds of galvanized spit.

Yet it *was* moving, raising (*a wax stump*) an arm, raising it in such a way that Amelia understood it had to be facing her after all, that the expressionless bumps and folds were its face.

Amelia cried out. She tried to stop her forward motion.

But the unseen waves propelled her.

How old?

Josh Malerman

Forever.

How old?

Never.

The shapeless thing raised its lumped arm high enough for Amelia to see it held (*no hands*) a black dress. As though Amelia had entered, had violated the privacy of someone getting dressed.

It can't see you, Amelia thought, with sudden clarity. *Turn around, Amelia! It doesn't know you're here!*

Amelia recalled the dining room. Reheard the creaking, the stretched (*wax*) footsteps from above.

It heard us. Couldn't see us. HEARD us.

The thing slid the billowing black fabric over its formless arms. Amelia imagined it in bed, asleep, as she and James lost their virginity below. She imagined it rising from its bed after hearing what sounded like love somewhere in the house.

We should introduce ourselves.

Yes. Still. Do it.

Because to *not* do it meant to leave the house and not to come back.

Amelia floated toward it.

Yes, she thought. *Tell it you're here. Tell it you live here now, too.*

When she was within reach, Amelia touched the thing's shoulder.

"I'm Amelia," she said. "Who are—"

And the lights went out.

Everywhere.

In the staggering darkness, Amelia reached for the wardrobe, but found nothing there. She lowered herself, stretching a flipper to the floor, but found nothing there.

She swam lower, deeper, but found nothing there.

And yet … a light far beneath her. A single small light, rising, growing larger, coming toward her until she understood that she was the object of that light, the very thing being sought.

Where are the stairs? Where is the floor?

The beam revealed (*it's gone, all of it, gone*) nothing.

No walls. No wood. No rugs, no windows, no chairs.

No more.

As James's light grew larger, brighter, Amelia looked everywhere for a sign of the house. A sign of the thing that lived there.

No more.

When James reached her, Amelia took his light and swam, spun, trying to find the house, their clubhouse, their (*Potscrubber*, James thought) their home.

105

When she trained the light back on James he was shaking his head no.

It's gone, he mouthed.

And it was.

Gone.

Just two teenagers now, swimming in the center of a very dark lake.

The house. No more.

34

It was wax, Amelia thought. *We could have shaped it into anything we wanted it to be.*

35

Amelia at home. On the couch. Thinking.

She thought a lot in the days following the final events at the house. She believed she knew what happened and why. But that was part of the problem; she was sick of asking why.

On one particularly motivated morning, she actually looked into it. Tried to find some information about the house. About the lake. A house at the bottom of a lake, she believed, *must* have a trail. Yet, there was nothing. No images, no stories, no rumors. And with every dead-end she met, she experienced a little relief. If nobody else had a story about the house ... didn't that mean that, in a way, it still belonged to Amelia and James? And if they never talked about it with anybody else, if they forever kept their secret, wouldn't it always remain theirs and theirs alone?

But that was the thing. One of the things. Many things. She *wanted* to talk about it with everybody she spoke to. Wanted to tell her parents. Tell her friends that she hadn't seen all summer because she was stuck on a boy, stuck on a raft tethered to a house in a lake. Stuck. Snagged. Trapped. She had to physically hold her mouth shut when her childhood friend Karrie called to ask how she'd been. Karrie knew something was amiss. Amelia could hear it in Karrie's questions. But there was no way Karrie could guess what it was, and so Amelia wasn't afraid. A drug addict might sniff. An alcoholic might smack her dry lips into the phone. But what did somebody who was stuck on a house sound like?

As long as nobody knew what it was, nobody could take it from her.

All this, Amelia believed, was, too much thinking. Way too much thinking. And yet, what else was she supposed to do? The house had vanished, leaving her and James floating in an empty lake, no more magical than any other lake in the world, except this one *had been* different; this one once harbored a house and in that house...

What?

Amelia closed her eyes.

James.

How was James?

They spoke in the few days following the final event at the house but it wasn't easy stuff. Both of them sounded dazed. There was too much space between their words. Long pauses at the end of their sentences. As if something was slowing them down, stretching their syllables, muting their meaning.

As if they were still talking underwater.

Amelia didn't tell James that she'd been hearing that same muted elongation everywhere. And that the doors in her house took longer to close than they should. Some seemed to sway shut on their own.

She opened her eyes.

James.

How *was* James?

They stopped talking after the first few days because it was just too weird. How many times could they say that was incredible, that was insane, what do we do now, what do we do now, what do we do now that we've experienced the apex of adventure and now have to face boring life ever after?

And how many times could they skirt the real issue, how freaky it had been, how unbelievably *scary?*

They didn't hang out. No spontaneous trips to the third lake. No scuba classes. No kisses. No firsts in a fully furnished house underwater.

How long had it been?

Ten days? Two weeks?

Amelia wasn't sure.

She checked her phone and saw nobody had called. Nobody had texted. Good. That way she didn't have to hold her mouth shut, didn't have to swallow the words that crawled up her throat, a description of the house, a recounting of the wonder that almost swallowed her whole.

We found a dangerously magic place. A place to fall in love.

She stared at the end of the couch, where she thought she saw the cushions ripple, for a moment, blurred by a mask she wasn't wearing, bubbles she didn't breathe.

But we lost it. And we don't know where it went.

Amelia shook these words out of her head. She turned on the television and felt sick with every image she saw. It all felt so practiced, so *dry* compared to what she and James had found.

And then lost.

She turned off the television. She closed her eyes.

James.

How was James now?

36

James couldn't sleep in his bedroom because it was still airing out from all the water damage. Two weeks later and it still smelled weird. Still smelled like a lake.

Dad was really on it, though. Really hell-bent on getting it back to normal. It had become a prideful project of his. James didn't mind. He was kind of glad to see Dad so obsessed. Made him feel better about his own obsessions.

Sleeping in the living room wasn't so bad. He had the T.V. for starters. But none of the movies were quite good enough. None of them matched the real life adventure he'd had. Action didn't thrill him like it used to. Like it was just a bunch of people dressed up as other people, pretending. Phony. The smell coming from his bedroom though, that was real. It didn't pretend. And the truth was, *everything* felt a little damp. His thoughts. His actions. The way everything rippled.

Even the shower smelled a bit like a lake. Like fish were swimming in the pipes.

James couldn't stop thinking about it. Didn't *want* to stop thinking about it. Kept recalling Amelia's voice, her expressions, the way she was on the third lake and especially inside the house. She was happy down there.

Was it his fault that they lost it?

He believed it was. The trouble probably started when he tried to remove the pepper shaker. He'd alerted someone to something. Pressed the wrong button. Knocked on the wrong door. Asked *how*.

These thoughts circulated like spinning tops as he sat on the back porch and thought about Amelia. He'd needed to get away from the lake smell. It wasn't that it was so bad, or so strong. In fact, it was because it was so faint, so far away, that it was close to driving him crazy.

The canoe was lying on its side in the grass. The way the dying sun hit it he could really see how much paint had been chipped off. The thing was practically silver now.

He remembered the overwhelming excitement of their first date. How scared he was to ask her. How incredible it was that she'd said yes.

He smiled. Not the half-smile of sadness, but the full, very real smile that comes with a good memory.

He pulled his phone from his pocket and called Amelia.

Could we ...

It rang.

What do you think about ...

And rang.

James wouldn't let himself believe it was going to voicemail. It couldn't. Not right now. Right now she had to pick up and they had to talk because, staring at the canoe, James was struck with a good idea. And because the idea was so good, and so true, Amelia must respond to it, must answer her phone, must sense that someone somewhere in the universe was trying to reach her with a good idea, must answer her phone and say

"Hello?"

"Amelia?"

"Yes."

"Hey."

"Hey, James."

"I was thinking."

"Me, too."

"Yeah?"

"Constantly. What were you thinking?"

"I was thinking we should go on a date."

Silence.

Then not.

"A date?"

"Yes. Dinner and a movie. A real first date."

Silence.

Then not.

"Okay."

"Yes?"

"Yes. How could I say no?"

Both seventeen. Both afraid. Both saying yes.

"Tomorrow? Late afternoon? Downtown?"

"Yes. Tomorrow. And James?"

"Yes?"

"I love you. I'm sorry I ruined it for us. I love you."

"What are you talking about? *I* ruined it for us!"

"No."

"No. *Yes.*"

"Wow," Amelia said. "Sounds like we had a similar week."

"Twelve days."

Amelia laughed. It sounded so good to hear her laugh.

"Tomorrow," she said. "A date."

"I'll pick you up and everything."

They hung up.

James tucked his phone into his pocket.

He started crying. Not out of sadness. Not really from happiness, either. It came from somewhere deeper. Somewhere completely submerged.

He cried and his tears felt sluggish, thicker than any tears he had cried before. Thick like water.

Like water from a lake.

37

They ate at the Chinese place on Simmer Street. They laughed a lot when Amelia accidentally walked into the men's room instead of the ladies'.

"They're not labeled right!" she said.

It was incredible. A reason to laugh. A real flub. On a real date.

They swapped stories about other first dates and James told Amelia about the lake smell in his house. Amelia told him that she felt like she was still underwater. Like she hadn't figured out how to be on land again. They talked about this a lot. Wondered aloud if that was how sailors felt, or the people who worked on cruise ships, once they finally came home after months at sea.

"Everything's a little wobbly," James said.

"I'm changed," Amelia said.

Some of it was heavy. Some of it wasn't. But it all felt good. Every syllable. Every beat. They were talking about things they'd wanted to talk about for days. *Days.* And doing it wasn't as hard as they thought it would be.

They laughed again when Amelia's fortune read: 'You will visit mysterious places.'

"That one's a little late," James said.

Amelia shrugged.

"Or not."

After they paid, on the way out, James smelled the same faint lake water smell from home. He brought his shirt to his nose.

Had to be that. But it wasn't.

They went to a movie but walked out halfway. Everybody in the theater was laughing hard and having a great time but they just couldn't get into it. Amelia used the word *transparent* and James thought that was a good word for it. And it wasn't just that they couldn't get into the story; it felt like they could see all the way *through* the story and there just wasn't any real magic to it.

So instead they walked. And they talked. And their talk remained fixed on heavier subjects because, no matter how much they joked about it, they'd been through something. They'd *seen* something. And they'd seen it together.

They walked away from downtown, to the darkening streets of the nicer homes, nicer than either of them had ever lived in. People were out on their porches. Some drank beer. Some smoked cigars.

Amelia and James walked.

Deeper.

Eventually their talk reached a subterranean level, an impossible pool in the basement of an impossible house. The roots. The place where the inexplicable grew, with no light to support it.

James felt it. Felt the growing space. The space between them getting larger, despite what they were trying to do.

"James," Amelia said, as they made another left, heading toward darker streets yet.

"What is it?" But he knew what it was.

Amelia stopped and faced him. Her features were obscured in the murky light.

"I think we need to end this. I think we peaked early and I think that, if we don't end it now, we're going to spend the rest of our lives talking about something that happened when we first met. One day, all of this will be a dream, partially a nightmare, and we'll feel bound to each other because of it. Because of something unreal that happened so long ago."

The growing space.

"I don't see why we have to end it, though," James said. But he did. He understood what Amelia was saying. It hurt was all.

"You'll be okay," Amelia said. "And I'll be okay."

A car drove by. To James it sounded like the engine was gargling. Like it was wet.

The waning light distorted Amelia's face just enough to make it appear as if she was wearing a plastic mask.

"Okay," James said.

Amelia reached out and squeezed both his hands.

James walked away.

Amelia walked the other way.

And as she walked, she thought about what she'd just done. It was right, she told herself. Had to be. Couldn't sit around for twelve more days thinking about a house that didn't exist. Couldn't spend the rest of her life talking about the time when she was seventeen.

She'd seen people like that. Mom and Dad's friends. Stuck. Snagged. Submerged.

She cried as she walked but she walked bravely. And every time she looked over her shoulder, looked to see if James was still standing where she left him, maybe even walking toward her, she saw only emptiness. Darkness. Like the areas of the lake the sun couldn't reach.

Fuck, Amelia thought. Fuck because it hurt. Fuck because she was right. Right? She was right to do what she did and James was right not to fight it.

They knew.

They both knew.

This was right.

The air grew colder and Amelia hugged herself, trying to fight it. Trying to stay warm and bright in a cool dark place.

Another right.

Another left.

The lighting was better here. The sun wasn't obscured by any of the downtown buildings. She looked over her shoulder.

James?

Did she want him to come for her?

She faced ahead again, facing the homes on the street.

One caught her attention. No lights on inside. But the shape of it. The size.

Amelia left the sidewalk, crossed the front lawn, went to the house.

At the front door, she pulled her phone from her pocket.

She called James.

"Hello?"

"James. Come to Chesterfield and Darcy," she was whispering, excitedly. Like she was whispering and screaming at once. "Come now."

"Amelia. We just—"

"I found it."

Silence. Then not.

"Found it?"

"The front door ... they fixed it ... someone fixed it ... and ... and ... there are three steps up to the front door, but you can tell ... you can tell what it was like before. Come now, James. Hurry."

"Chesterfield and Darcy."

"*Yes.* Oh my God, James. Oh my God the windows. The roof. Come *now.*"

Amelia hung up. She backed up from the front door, backed up far enough so that she was able to see it all at once.

She fell to her knees on the lawn.

The feeling she had wasn't happiness. Wasn't relief.

It was different.

Deeper.

"James!" she cried out, smiling. "I found it!"

Far away, as if muted by layers of water, unseen waves, she heard footsteps on the concrete sidewalk. The thud-drumming, drum-thudding of James coming to see it for himself.

"I found it!" she yelled.

She felt the growing space, too. But not the space between her and James. Rather, the space *beyond* them, as if the two of them were the world and all else stretched, receded, became a shoreline, too far to see.

Amelia closed her eyes.

She opened them.

The lights had come on. Inside the house. The lights had come on.

James was getting closer. She could hear his shoes on the sidewalk, could hear him calling from somewhere in the same endless body of water.

"Amelia!" he called. Closer. "Where is it?"

"That one," she said, pointing now, not sure if he could hear her. That was okay. He would see for himself in a moment. Finding a good place just took a little navigation. "That one," she said. "Where the lights have come on ..."

ALSO FROM THIS IS HORROR